"Kiss me,"

Emma's heart pounded hard. *Bad idea.*

He had the audacity to smile at her. She felt his gaze on her like a brand. It slid over her breasts and stomach, and her insides tightened with an unwanted but impossible-to-ignore desire.

"See, I *knew* you knew words other than *no*, Em."

"I need to get out of here." But she didn't move. They were alone in the library of Xavier Franklin's mansion with a party going on outside the heavy closed doors. She could hear the voices, the laughter, the band playing some classical number.

"So, you're still maintaining that you hate me," Ryan said.

She nodded. "I can't stand you."

"But you want me."

Unfortunately, yes. *Damn it.*

It was Emma who closed the distance between them. Her mind was foggy, but her body knew what it wanted. It wanted Ryan. It had wanted Ryan since almost the first moment she'd met him. And the lust potion, just a small splash of it, had heightened that need inside of her to an uncontrollable level.

Just because it was inconvenient didn't mean it wasn't true.

Dear Reader,

I think some things are *Inevitable*.

When Emma and Ryan—both agents for the Paranormal Investigation and Recovery Agency—met, it was difficult for them to keep their hands off each other. But between maintaining their self-control and holding on to a friendship they found too valuable to risk destroying with a fling, things just didn't work out. As they meet again after six months apart, the sparks fly...but they still have those pesky walls getting in the way of their happiness.

That's why I'm here! (evil laugh) I like to give my reluctant characters a little push in the right direction. For Emma and Ryan, I chose a lust potion. Instead of waiting for things to happen naturally, they fall into each other's arms...and bed!

Between misunderstandings, magic potions, heartbroken ghosts, stolen goods and masquerade parties, I think they just might find their way toward their very sexy—and *inevitable*—happily ever after!

I hope you enjoy Emma and Ryan's story as much as I enjoyed writing it. Please visit my website anytime at www.michellerowen.com. I love hearing from readers!

Happy reading!

Michelle Rowen

Michelle Rowen

INEVITABLE

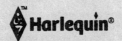

TORONTO NEW YORK LONDON
AMSTERDAM PARIS SYDNEY HAMBURG
STOCKHOLM ATHENS TOKYO MILAN MADRID
PRAGUE WARSAW BUDAPEST AUCKLAND

Recycling programs
for this product may
not exist in your area.

ISBN-13: 978-0-373-79604-5

INEVITABLE

Copyright © 2011 by Michelle Rowen

www.eHarlequin.com

Printed in U.S.A.

ABOUT THE AUTHOR

National bestselling author Michelle Rowen writes all sorts of paranormal romance—light and dark, sexy and sweet, and has won an *RT Book Reviews* Reviewers' Choice Award and a Holt Medallion for her work. A voracious but picky reader, TV viewer and movie watcher, she prefers all her entertainment to include a happily ever after...or else! Michelle lives in Southern Ontario. *Inevitable* is her third foray into the marvelously sexy fictional world that is Harlequin Blaze. Please visit her online at www.michellerowen.com.

Books by Michelle Rowen
HARLEQUIN BLAZE
503—HOT SPELL
578—TOUCH AND GO

For Eve, Jackie, Jill, Michele, Charlene, and Megan.
Write on, ladies!

1

"I'D BET YOU'VE NEVER SEEN one this big before, have you?"

Emma Black forced a smile to her face. "Wow. It's *really* big."

"Thank you, my dear." Eighty-year-old billionaire Xavier Franklin gently placed the eighteen-inch-tall antique perfume bottle on a shelf along with other examples of his priceless glassware collection. The brightly lit glass and chrome showroom felt more like something out of a museum than one that would be found in a private home. "But enough about my hobbies, I've been monopolizing your time for far too long. You likely want to get back to the party, don't you?"

No. What Emma really wanted was to get her hands on the potion bottle she'd been sent here, to New York City, to retrieve. When she'd arrived at Franklin's twelve-thousand-square-foot mansion on Central Park West, it had seemed like such a simple assignment.

That had been two hours ago.

She'd arrived to find one of Franklin's infamous masquerade parties going on. She'd read about them before—glitzy events put on by a man who still thought of himself as one of the city's most eligible bachelors. With a lot of time on his hands and a ton of money at his disposal, his parties had become the place for the most beautiful and important people in the Manhattan social scene to meet up, drink fountains of champagne, and— Well, whatever happened, happened.

And here she was, being given the grand tour by the eighty-year-old bachelor himself. She supposed she should feel honored. There weren't a lot of glitzy parties in Mystic Ridge, the town where she lived, unless you counted going for a few drinks at the local bar.

Since Emma had arrived sans costume, she'd been handed a mask at the door. The billionaire also wore a mask, a green one with a large feather.

"Actually, Mr. Franklin—" she said, wanting to move things along.

"Please, my dear. Call me Xavier."

It was obvious he'd had a few too many glasses of champagne. He grinned at her like a tipsy teenager, the deep wrinkles fanning out around his eyes.

Maybe he needed a little direction to remember the task at hand. "Xavier…you called us, remember? I'm here to pick up your potion bottle and take it back to PARA."

PARA was an acronym for the Paranormal Assessment and Recovery Agency, of which Emma was an agent. She assessed. She recovered. Since her psychic ability was clairvoyance, she sometimes spoke to ghosts to help direct them on to the next plane of existence— kind of like a supernatural flight attendant. Some of the ghosts even listened to her.

If someone had something they believed was enchanted or cursed, PARA would send an agent to check it out. If it was determined to be dangerous, the article in question would be kept under lock and key in the vault until it could be disenchanted, decursed or destroyed.

PARA was a privately funded business and Xavier was one of its biggest benefactors. Basically, whatever Xavier wanted, PARA provided for him. He'd just acquired a rare bottle of potion, but the potion wasn't working as he'd been told it would. He wanted it assessed to see if he'd been duped into buying a fake. It wasn't an important or a dangerous job. It was simply time-consuming. Since her car was in the shop, the bus ride from Mystic Ridge to New York City had taken three hours.

Yes, Xavier Franklin always got what he wanted. He'd, in fact, requested Emma by name after they'd met at a fundraising cocktail party a few months ago put on by the PARA board of directors. She was trying to take it as a compliment, even if it meant she was being used as a glorified courier.

Xavier's cell phone buzzed and he pulled it from his pocket. "Yes, the bottle. Of course. I'll get it for you in a moment, my dear. In the meantime, please enjoy yourself. Have some champagne."

He wandered off with his phone pressed to his ear, the enormous peacock feather set into his mask flopping around at the top of it with every step he took.

The shoes Emma wore pinched her feet. Since she'd always disliked how short she was—all of five-foot-one—she never left her apartment without high heels, the higher the better. This pair had been on sale for a price she couldn't resist, but she'd been paying the real price for her frugality every minute since she'd put them on.

"Such a glamorous life," she said under her breath as her gaze moved over the hundreds of colorful glass bottles, vases and bowls lit up and displayed on shelves and tabletops. The main party was being held in the parlor at the front of the house with a two-storey-high ceiling, a dome-shaped skylight, and a chandelier so large and grand that it likely would impress even the Phantom of the Opera.

The Franklin Mansion, considered a pre-war historic home, was at least 150 years old—old enough that Emma was surprised no other phantoms were wandering around. It was a good thing she didn't sense anything otherworldly. She wasn't there for an exorcism, just a simple courier job.

While she was in Manhattan, though, she'd decided to take care of some other business. Along with being a paranormal investigator, Emma had a bit of a sideline going that very few people knew about. She was a writer. An author, in fact. She'd written an erotic novel and it had just been published a week ago.

It was her naughty little secret—a bit like wearing black lace panties and garters under an old pair of jeans.

Her editor was thrilled with *Inevitable,* a book she'd written under a pseudonym and she'd asked Emma to swing by the office today for a quick visit, during which she'd given Emma a stack of extra copies of the release. She wanted to offer Emma a contract to write more, but Emma wasn't sure she had more books in her. The only reason she'd written *this* book was because she'd had a certain set of fantasies that wouldn't let go of her imagination until she'd put them down on paper. Now they were down. They were published. And Emma felt she should focus on her career with PARA. After all, that's what paid the bills.

If she'd known she'd have to lug a dozen books in a tote bag around a masquerade party for hours on end, she might have stashed them in a locker somewhere until it was time to head back home. Within the next hour, she needed to grab Xavier's bottle and then catch her bus back to Mystic Ridge at eleven o'clock.

But then, out of the corner of her eye, she saw a familiar face.

It felt as if someone had just punched her in her gut.

Ryan Shephard.

"Son of a bitch," she whispered. What the hell was *he* doing here?

Her eyes narrowed. As if she had to ask. There were tens of millions of dollars worth of art and collectibles under this roof.

It was the perfect place for a thief like Ryan.

She moved to the archway between the rooms and watched as he slowly made his way through the crowd, pausing to chat with the other masked party-goers as if he belonged there when it was obvious to her he'd crashed. He'd never get an invitation to a fancy event like this one with his reputation.

Even with the red mask that covered half his face, she'd recognize him anywhere. The line of his jaw. The shape of his lips. The way his tall, chiseled frame filled out that black tuxedo.

She bit her bottom lip. Just because the man had betrayed her, lied to her, and walked away without even trying to explain himself, that didn't mean she still didn't find him painfully attractive.

It had been six months since her former partner at PARA had been caught stealing from the vault, intending to sell the enchanted objects and treasures within to private buyers.

They'd been partners for a year. Friends. Confidants. They'd laughed together, shared secrets, and gotten to know each other very well. Too well. Along the way, Emma had felt something much stronger than friendship for Ryan growing inside her. Just as she was gaining the courage she needed to act on it, he began dating her friend Charlotte.

Emma took that as the hint that he saw them as just friends, although the fantasies about him that plagued her were difficult to deal with. Constant. Erotic. Distracting. They were the same ones she'd needed to get down on paper, exorcizing them from her mind as if they were pesky ghosts.

She'd thought those fantasies were long gone now, captured on the page. But one look at Ryan had brought them all flooding back to her.

How annoying.

There'd also been another man she'd once trusted with all her heart before he betrayed her. Her father. He'd been a gambling addict and alcoholic who'd taken off and left her and her mother far behind when Emma had been in her late teens. No excuses, no apologies. He was just gone.

Then ten years later, Ryan had worked his way under her skin. She felt comfortable with him in a way that she'd never felt with other men—coworkers *or* boyfriends. And just when she'd been ready to put absolute trust in him, he'd shattered it in one fell swoop.

Ryan Shephard was a liar and a thief. Just because he was also drop dead sexy did nothing to help balance the scales. The last time they'd spoken, she believed she'd said something like: "I never want to see you again, you bastard."

Perhaps she hadn't been quite as polite, but that had been the gist of it. He'd been using her all along, trying to get into the good graces and trust of a long-time PARA agent like her, so he could get access to the office after hours.

And he'd lied about it by saying he hadn't done anything wrong. Then he'd turned tail and left Mystic Ridge without another word.

He *had* done it. She had no doubt about that. If he'd just owned up to it, admitted he'd made the wrong choice... then *maybe* she might feel differently about the entire situation. Be he hadn't. And that just made her think about the father who'd run away from a tough situation, with no regard for a wife and daughter who would have stood by him, no matter what.

Bad memories. Very bad.

Emma was surprised that seeing Ryan again affected her so much. Suddenly her palms were moist and her heart pounded like a jackhammer.

She was at the party to do her job and retrieve the potion bottle from Xavier, nothing else. Still, if Ryan Shephard was at this party, she was sure he was up to no good.

Summoning up her courage, she put one heel-clad foot in front of the other and made a beeline toward him. A waiter carrying a tray of champagne passed by and she grabbed a glass, downing it in one gulp before she carried on. Her borrowed mask felt hot and uncomfortable.

The faces around her were all covered in masks as well. Behind them, she knew she'd find local politicians, socialites, businesspeople, and a few celebrities. She didn't pay them any attention. She ignored the classical music coming from the corner of the opulent ballroom. The four string quartet also wore masks. Emma's eyes were solely fixed on her target.

Thief.

Liar.

Heartbreaker.

The star of her most erotic fantasies.

Ryan was bad news. And bad news was best thrown in the trash or used to line a bird cage.

He was talking to a buxom blonde wearing a pink feathered mask to match her tight pink cocktail dress when Emma tapped him on the shoulder. His back stiffened and he glanced at her.

"Hi there," he said with a slow smile.

She cocked her head. "Hi there? Really?"

He turned back to the blonde. "Sorry."

"Not a problem," she demurred. "I'll catch up with you later. You have my phone number."

"Yes, I do. Thanks for that."

"My pleasure."

Oh, brother. Emma crossed her arms and tapped her foot as she waited for the blonde to wander off. Finally, he turned back to face her. The cobalt-blue eyes she remembered all too clearly were jarring behind his mask as he leisurely scanned her from head to toe. He ran a hand through his jet-black hair. It was a little longer than it had been the last time she'd seen him.

The smile he gave her was enough to melt her panties. That is, if he really affected her anymore. And, unfortunately, he did. Unexpected desire, much like a surge of electricity jolted through her.

Not helpful.

"Well?" she prompted, wanting some sort of explanation about why he was there and what he was up to.

"Are you enjoying yourself?" he asked casually.

She stared at him for a moment. "Pardon me?"

"It's a great party, isn't it? The food is incredible. Have you been to the rooftop terrace yet?" He glanced toward the spiral staircase. "The view of Central Park is spectacular from up there."

She gaped at him in disbelief. After everything that had happened, every case they'd investigated together, every hour they'd spoken in the past, every sexual fantasy she'd secretly harbored for him—he didn't know who she was under her mask.

Of all the damned nerve.

RYAN WRACKED HIS MIND for the right movie quote. It was from Casablanca and Bogie had said it. Something about a whole lot of gin joints in the world and Ingrid Bergman had to walk into his.

He wasn't Humphrey Bogart and this wasn't an old movie. But the sight of beautiful Emma Black immediately made him want to head to the bar in the corner of the parlor and consume a great deal of gin.

Even with a party mask on, he would recognize her anywhere. And not just because of her long flame-red hair—although it did help her stand out in a crowd. She was short in stature—not much over five feet, but she always made up for it by wearing treacherously high heels. Tonight she wore a simple black dress, a little less fancy and shiny than what other women were wearing tonight, but he had to fight his gaze not to skim down her body again. He thought he'd memorized every luscious curve back when they were partners, but unexpectedly seeing her standing right in front of him had been enough to knock all logical thought out of his head.

No, it wasn't just because of her hair or her body that he recognized her.

It was the look in her emerald green eyes. He remembered that look after being on the receiving end of it nearly six months ago.

Sheer unadulterated hatred.

It brought back memories—bad ones.

His knee-jerk reaction to seeing her standing there glaring at him like he was an insect that had the audacity to smash into her windshield was to pretend he didn't recognize her.

And here they were.

"Anyway—" he pushed a facsimile of a charming smile to his lips "—have a lovely evening."

He didn't want to scurry off with his tail between his legs, but the compulsion was strong.

"Ryan," she said sharply. "It's *me*."

This ruse wasn't going to last. But owning up to it right away just wasn't in his nature. "Have we met before?"

"Yes." It was more of a hiss than a confirmation.

He scratched his chin. "You do seem a bit familiar to me. Was it Hawaii? A little bar called the Lotus Flower?"

The glare she gave him was sharp enough to wound. "You're hilarious."

"I am known for my sense of humor."

"What the hell are you doing here, Ryan?" There was a decidedly unpleasant edge to her words that tasted a bit to him like venom. She had just as much of a sense of humor as he did—at least she *used* to. It was one of the things he liked best about her. This, however, was not one of those times she chose to tap into it.

Ryan's smile finally faded. "Emma."

Her eyes widened. "Ha! I *knew* you recognized me."

"Long time no see."

"Not long enough. Why are you here?"

He glanced around. "I'm attending a party."

"With or without an invitation?"

One thing he'd learned about the delicious Emma

Black, after working side by side with her for a year—she never minced words. Tact was not always at the top of her to-do list either. "What are *you* doing here?" he countered.

"You didn't answer my question."

"You're right, I didn't." He eyed a couple who passed them on the way to the open bar. "I do have an invite, although it wasn't necessarily sent to me personally. Perhaps you'd like to alert security that I'm crashing and have them drag me out. Would that make you feel good about yourself?"

"It might."

He forced a smile. "Don't worry your pretty little head. I'm not up to anything nefarious."

"I find that hard to believe."

He held out his hand. "Let's put the past behind us, Emma."

She eyed his hand as if it were covered in fungus. "Right, like I'm going to touch you so you can get a read on me."

All agents with PARA, current and former, were psychic. The majority were either empathic—those able to sense emotions and feelings from other people through touch—or clairvoyant—those able to communicate with ghosts and sense important things from objects or places without relying on the usual five senses.

In their partnership, Ryan was the people person and Emma dealt with all the other stuff. His empathic ability had never been very strong and he had to work hard to get any kind of reading at all. He also had to do it through skin to skin contact. Some empaths were strong enough to get a sense of another just from being in the same room with them. Not Ryan. He was a one on a scale of one to five, maybe a two on a good day. His gift was more like strong intuition rather than total psychic ability. But he'd made it work for himself and his low-end ability had never really given him any problems on the job.

He was much better with cars, really. Tinkering with cars, sensing what made them work—or not work—was his true talent. And his true love. It wasn't related to his psychic ability, but it might as well have been. He felt he had a sixth sense about cars. But that hadn't been put to much use as a PARA agent.

One thing he had going for himself as an empath was that other empaths couldn't get a read on him. This was both a blessing and a curse since it meant that his secrets remained secrets.

"Read you?" He gave her an innocent look. "I wouldn't do something shady like that without your permission."

"You don't need to read me. I can tell you what I'm feeling—disgusted. And a little nauseous."

"The shrimp pâté *is* a bit questionable. I'd stay away from the caviar as well. Nasty stuff."

Her cheeks went a bit flushed. He was surprised that he seemed to be able to affect her just with a few words. She must really hate him, even after all this time.

He wished the feeling was mutual.

Since he'd been fired from PARA for theft, he'd worked a lot of jobs to make ends meet. In a week he was scheduled to move down to Florida to work with his brother in a high-end garage taking care of luxury vehicles. It was a dream job for him.

However, he had a little bit of business to clear up first before he left.

Emma looked up at him. He was six-two, so even with the highest heels she was still at a height disadvantage. But what she lacked in stature, she made up for in attitude. Their gazes locked and he felt something stir inside him. Desire. He found her just as gorgeous as he ever had and she affected him whether he liked it or not. It put him at an extreme disadvantage if he was trying to keep his cool.

"If you try to steal anything from Xavier Franklin tonight," she said slowly and evenly, "there will be consequences. I don't know how you managed to get your hands on an invitation, but the security for this party is very tight. PARA didn't press charges when you stole from them, but Xavier would."

Now that was a low blow. What happened six months ago was still constantly on his mind. He didn't need the reminder.

Ryan's mood darkened as if a storm cloud had drifted overhead. "No, PARA didn't press charges. After all, who's going to believe a self-proclaimed supernatural investigation agency that says they're missing a stash of enchanted tea cups or grandfather clocks? I know the board of directors likes to keep PARA business private."

"All I'm saying—"

"I get it, Emma. Stealing is wrong."

Her fierce expression faltered. "I don't know why I'm even talking to you. I washed my hands of you a long time ago."

"I remember." Her words made something sharp and painful twist in his chest. He'd valued their friendship more than she ever knew. Enough that he'd started casually dating another woman, Charlotte, when he began developing deeper feelings for Emma. It had made sense at the time. His relationships—they didn't last long. They never had. And if he'd had a fling with Emma, it would have ended the friendship he valued so much. A friendship that ended anyway. Maybe it had never been as strong as he would have liked to believe.

He pushed the grin back onto his face, though it felt as false as it probably looked. "Don't worry about me, Em. I have things under control. Enjoy the party."

Ryan turned to walk up the stairs to the terrace. He was now in desperate need of some fresh air. Emma thought he was a thief who'd manipulated her and shamelessly lied to her. That he was the sort of man who would steal potentially dangerous items and sell them for profit. Your average enchanted tea cup went for a whole lot of green on the black market and there were literally hundreds of eager buyers worldwide who had vast collections of supernatural paraphernalia hidden away in their mansions. It was a booming business.

But there was a big problem with Emma's theory. Despite what she believed, he'd never stolen anything from PARA's vaults.

Never.

The evidence, however, proved otherwise and had gotten him swiftly fired without a chance to properly plead his case. Since he was an empath—even a low-end one—there was no way to gauge if he was telling the truth when he'd denied the charges.

Ryan knew he'd been set up. And his life and career had been ruined because of it.

That was why he'd come here tonight. He'd crashed Xavier Franklin's ritzy masquerade party because he suspected the billionaire was one of those supernatural collectors. If he could find hard evidence of that fact, he might discover who'd been providing Franklin, and others like him, with merchandise.

Ryan was all ready to start his new life down in Florida at a job he knew he was going to love. But first, something deep inside of him was driving him to clear his name. Otherwise this stain on his character would never let him rest. He didn't want distractions or regrets to haunt him as he embarked on his future.

And yes, he wanted to prove to Emma Black, once and for all, that he wasn't a thief. That he wasn't a liar. He wanted to see that trust in her eyes again one last time before he walked away and never looked back. He wanted her to feel sorry that she ever doubted him in the first place.

She'd been totally wrong about him and he'd prove it.

However, based on their latest little confrontation, he knew that was going to be one hell of an uphill battle.

2

AN HOUR LATER, Emma sat on the stiff, black leather couch in the library where she'd been told to wait for Xavier and tried not to think about what happened with Ryan.

She tried. She wasn't all that successful.

One brief conversation and he was suddenly all she could think about. Maybe she should seek him out again and get more answers from him. Or maybe she should keep trying to forget she ever saw him in the first place.

Finally, Xavier entered the room. "There you are, my dear."

She stood up. Her purse and tote bag full of books leaned against the leg of the couch to her left. "Here I am. Do you have it?"

"I certainly do."

He held a small green glass bottle. It was about the size of an antique perfume bottle with a glass stopper.

"It's beautiful," she said.

"I acquired it in London a few months ago." He looked at it sourly. "I'm disappointed in it."

It was half filled with liquid. "What sort of potion is it supposed to be?"

"It is called *Desidero*." He peered at it through the opening in his mask. "It's supposed to be a mood enhancer, but it doesn't seem to work at all. I've tested it several times to no avail, which leads me to believe I was either duped when I bought it or its properties are no longer viable. I spent a great deal of money on this and if PARA determines that it is not what it is meant to be, then those who sold it to me will be held accountable. At the very least, I'll expect my money back."

"Is it dangerous?"

"Not at all. Like I said, it doesn't work. It's no more dangerous than water."

Emma took the bottle from him and inspected it, turning it around in her hand. The stopper didn't look particularly snug. She'd brought a sealed case to keep it in for the trip back so no contents would spill. "We're happy to assess it for you and let you know what we find. It'll probably take about a week before someone gives you the report. Anyway, it was very nice to meet you, Xavier."

She was about to move past him to grab her bags when he blocked her path. "Leaving so soon?" he asked.

"I appreciate you letting me attend the party, but I think it's time I headed home. My bus leaves at eleven and it's already ten o'clock."

"I understand," he said, nodding. "But if you're tired, I have plenty of room here at my mansion. I could have a bed made up for you."

"That's really not necessary."

He drew closer to her. "I'd love the chance to get to know you better."

Emma stiffened as she felt his bony hand press against

her. "Are you aware that you're now cupping my right breast?"

He smiled. "Such a lovely right breast it is. The left one is equally alluring."

Oh, boy. "I need to go now."

"I'm a very rich man, Emma. And I enjoy collecting beautiful things. I have three mistresses set up in Manhattan, two in Toronto, and one in London. Have you ever given any thought to letting someone take care of you so you can live a life of leisure rather than having to pursue a full-time career to support yourself?"

She eyed him. "Are you asking me to be one of your mistresses?"

He swept his gaze over her, stopping at her cleavage. "I don't have a redhead in my collection yet."

She couldn't say she was overly surprised by this turn of events. Xavier Franklin's reputation for chasing much younger women by the baker's dozen did precede him, after all. She was surprised he only had six mistresses.

"Look, Xavier, I'm flattered, of course, but I wouldn't say I'm in the market for—"

He aimed a kiss toward her mouth, but she dodged out of the way just in time. He grinned wickedly at her. "I like a little spunk in my ladies. The chase only makes it more fun!"

This wasn't happening to her. "I really need to leave."

His pale eyes swept over her body. "You, me, hot tub. Now. You can leave the mask on but everything else comes off. I enjoy a bit of mystery."

She grimaced. "No, thanks."

"Your beautiful lips say no, but your sexy green eyes say yes."

"My sexy green eyes are also saying no. Trust me on that."

He grabbed her wrist and she had to jostle to keep a hold of the potion bottle so it wouldn't spill. "I've desired you since the moment we met. I want to make love to you."

She gritted her teeth. "That wasn't part of the agreement with PARA."

"I don't care." He waved a hand flippantly. "You know, Emma, I have a difficult time taking no for an answer."

"I can see that." She didn't want to resort to kneeing the old man in his privates, but it was a distinct possibility she'd have to go there. He was rich and powerful. PARA considered him a VIP, so he could make her life very difficult, but she'd be damned if she was going to let him to fondle her like one of his shiny glass bowls.

"Excuse me," a familiar voice said from behind them. "Emma, I was wondering where you'd gotten to. Is everything okay?"

She turned with shock to see Ryan standing by the open door to the library.

"Who are you?" Xavier demanded, without letting go of her wrist.

"I don't think we've been formally introduced. I'm Ryan. Emma's fiancé." He smiled thinly. "Is there a problem here?"

Xavier let go of her so abruptly she nearly stumbled backward. She pressed her hand over the top of the bottle to keep the stopper in place.

"Emma, I wasn't aware that you were engaged," he said.

Her first inclination was to deny it, but she bit her tongue long enough to come to her senses. "Oh, yes.

Very engaged. Ryan came along with me tonight. It was a long drive and I wanted the company."

"Yes," Ryan agreed. "I couldn't let my angel come all this way by herself. The city can be very dangerous. Predators are everywhere. Present company excluded, of course."

Xavier pursed his lips. "I thought you said you were taking the bus back tonight."

"I...uh, yes, of course," she said. "We both took the bus."

The billionaire eyed each of them in turn and Emma was certain he didn't believe a word they spoke.

"Yes, well," he finally relented. "I really must get back to my party. Everyone will be wondering where I've gotten to."

"Good idea," Ryan said. "Bye now."

"Lovely to meet you. Both of you." Without another word, Xavier Franklin left the library and closed the heavy, ornately carved door behind him, leaving Emma and Ryan alone. She finally released the breath she'd been holding.

"You don't have to thank me—" Ryan offered.

She looked at him, trying her best to repress the gratitude she felt. "I wasn't going to."

"—but you're welcome."

Emma put her hand on her hip. "I could have handled that, you know."

"A dirty old man with big bucks trying to get you into his hot tub? Yeah, you probably could have. But I thought I'd intervene, just for old time's sake. You do know these parties are simply a way for him to meet new women, right?" His gaze narrowed on the bottle she held. "So, what's that?"

"A bottle."

"I figured that part out all by myself. Was it a gift from the octogenarian Casanova?"

"Not a gift. I'm taking it back to PARA with me. Don't try to steal it or I might be forced to stab you in the eyeball."

He raised a dark brow. "With what?"

Emma frowned. "I have a very pointy pencil in my purse and I know how to use it."

He studied her for a moment. "I see. So if you're here on behalf of my old employer, where's your new partner?"

"I don't have a partner at the moment. I'm currently working independently."

"For six long months?" His lips stretched over his straight white teeth. "So nobody lived up to me, did they?"

She shook her head. "I see you haven't misplaced your inflated ego anywhere."

"Thought I did for a while, but I found it in my sock drawer."

Speaking with the gorgeous but disappointing man in front of her was wearying, especially when being close to him made it difficult to separate the anger she felt from the desire that pooled inside her. It was well past the time when Emma wanted to leave. "Well, it's been great walking down memory lane with you, Ryan, but time is a-fleeting." She grabbed her purse, slung it over her shoulder, and then eyed the tote bag. She'd have to catch a cab to the bus station. Any more walking was out of the question tonight with this load. All she knew was she had to escape. And soon.

His smile faded. "So you're going to leave, just like that."

She shrugged. "My work here is done. I have what I came for and now it's time for me to go."

He'd drawn close enough that she could feel his body heat. She forced herself not to back up a step or show any weakness toward him.

"Take off your mask, Em. I want to see your face," he said.

"No."

"Is that the only word you know?"

"Tonight it is."

She wanted to stay professional, but it was difficult when Ryan Shephard was so close to her. She'd tried very hard to forget about him, to put everything that happened between them well behind her. Logically, she knew she wasn't supposed to like him anymore, but it was as if her body had a mind of its own.

A whole year of wanting him when they worked together, side by side. Never having him. Fantasies of bare skin, his body pressed to hers, his lips and tongue moving over her naked body, lower, lower...

She had to get out of here.

"Can I tell you a secret, Em?" he asked after a moment.

"I'd prefer than you don't. And stop calling me Em." Her grip tightened on the bottle of potion. It was an abbreviation of her name that he'd used in the past, but now it felt much too intimate.

His jaw tightened. "Fine, *Emma*. Then let me ask you a question first."

She reached up to adjust her mask. Flimsy though it was, it felt like it offered her a bit of protection against the man facing her. "Go ahead. But I can't guarantee I'm going to answer it."

"When you heard that I'd stolen all that stuff from the vaults, did it ever occur to you that I didn't do it?"

"No," she said, hating that her throat now felt thick. She didn't want him to affect her like this. She thought she'd steeled herself against him a long time ago.

His blue eyes grew serious beneath his red mask. "Why not?"

"Because there was a witness to your actions, someone I trust more than anyone in the world."

His eyes narrowed. "Who?"

"Like I'm going to tell you." A flare of anger ignited inside her, which helped her see things clearly again. "Look, Ryan, I don't care if you're only now starting to feel guilt about what happened. I don't care if you're looking to make amends. It's too late for that."

"So you still hate me."

She blew out a breath. "Actually, I feel nothing for you."

His face tightened. "That's even worse."

"Just because you're having a moment of guilt doesn't mean I need to feel sorry for you. It's not going to happen. You made your choices and I made mine."

"Did you ever feel anything for me?" He searched her face.

Dangerous question. "You're the empath. You tell me."

His lips curved at the edges. "Humor me."

Humor him. She wasn't sure why she would want to do something like that.

"Okay, you really want to know?" She exhaled shakily and her grip on the glass bottle tightened until the sharp edges bit into her skin. "Whatever I might have felt for you in the past was swept away the moment you decided that being my partner at PARA was not as good as making some easy cash on the side. You had a good life and some great friends—especially me—and you threw it all away. We knew each other a year, Ryan. You were my partner. I trusted you with—" Her voice caught and she cleared her throat. "Quite honestly, at this very moment I just want you to go away and stay gone. I really never wanted to see you again."

The words poured out of her mouth in a gush and he stood there letting her have her say. The look on his face, although partially hidden, stiffened with every word she uttered. His reaction bothered her, she couldn't help it.

Because, bottom line, six months ago—even after he started dating Charlotte—she'd been well on her way to falling in love with him. And he'd broken her heart. So she'd stuffed those feelings down deep and tried not to pay any attention to them. But seeing him tonight—the realization that she was far from over him was not a comfort in any way, shape, or form. Actually, it made her want to cry.

Finally, a glimmer of a smile, although now lacking any humor, touched Ryan's lips. "I guess it can't get much more clear than that, can it?"

She swallowed past the lump in her throat. "You said you had a secret you wanted to tell me?"

"Forget it. Suddenly I'm not in much of a mood for sharing."

"Then I'm going to go. Goodbye, Ryan."

"Goodbye, Emma."

She took a deep breath and began to walk past him. She had a feeling that after tonight, she'd never see him again. It would be for the best—for both of them.

"Wait…before you go—" He reached out and grabbed her wrist to stop her. The bottle Xavier had given her earlier jerked and the loose-fitting top flew off. The clear, oily liquid within spilled over the lip of the bottle and splashed them both.

"Damn." She rubbed her hand against her dress, then grabbed for the stopper and quickly put it back in place.

"What is that stuff?" Ryan asked. He brought his fingers to his temples as if he'd suddenly developed a headache.

The temperature in the room felt as if it had just shot up about twenty degrees. A wave of dizziness swept through her. She pressed her hand to her face. "PARA business. It's the reason I'm here in the first place."

He frowned. "So that means it's not just any bottle. What's inside of it?"

"Xavier said it was something he'd gotten in London. Some sort of mood enhancing potion, but it doesn't work properly. He called it Desidero."

He gaped at her. "Did you say *Desidero?*"

The look of surprise on his face didn't help calm her nerves. "Yes."

He grimaced. "Uh, oh."

She stared at him. "Uh, oh, what?"

"You're sure that's what he said? Desidero potion?"

"Positive, but he says it doesn't work. You know what it is?"

"I worked a few weeks in the potions division when I started at the agency, before I was assigned as your partner. It was part of my training. Desidero was one of the potions I learned about." He looked at the bottle she held. "Mood enhancement, huh? I guess it'll kick in any second now."

"What will kick in?"

He shook his head. "A whole lot of trouble."

"He said it didn't work properly."

"Oh, it's working, all right. I can feel it right now." He rubbed his temples again.

Her entire body felt flushed. Maybe she was having an allergic reaction to it. "Do I have to get violent to make you spit out what you know?"

Ryan hissed out a breath through his teeth. "It's a lust potion, Emma. An old one from the British Isles. There's a legend that says that this is the potion that Guinevere was given to make her fall in love with King Arthur, but it didn't work quite that smoothly. You know what happened with Lancelot, right? She fell for him instead. It's this potion's fault. And, no, it doesn't work on everyone which is why Franklin thought it was a dud. Some mood enhancer. He has no idea."

Her mouth dropped open. "Guinevere and Lancelot?"

"You got it."

A lust potion. That would explain why she suddenly felt so warm. Why her body had begun to tingle. Why her nipples had tightened. Why her belly twisted with a strange and difficult to ignore need. Why she desperately wanted Ryan's hands on her as soon as possible. "Lustful for...?"

He smiled, but it was shaky. "Well, I guess that would be *me*."

"You?"

"We were together when it spilled on us." His gaze, now heated, swept her body as he drew closer. "It's rare and dangerous stuff."

A shiver went down her spine. "There's some left. If you stole it, you could get a lot of money for something like this."

"I could. *If* I stole it."

Her breath came quick, and Ryan's mouth was sud-

denly the main focus of her entire world. "I feel an irresistible need to kiss you right now. Which is incredibly
inconvenient considering how much I hate you," she
whispered.

"I thought you said you were indifferent to me. Put
down the bottle before you break it. If any more of that
stuff spills, we might have a larger problem to deal with
here."

Instead of arguing, she placed the green glass bottle
down on a table next to the couch and dropped her purse
to the floor. "So…now what do we do?"

She felt his gaze on her like a brand. It slid over her
breasts and stomach, and her insides tightened with
desire.

"Kiss me," he suggested.

Her heart pounded hard. "Bad idea."

"You're afraid what might happen?"

"Yes."

He had the audacity to smile at her. "See, I *knew* you
knew words other than no, Em."

"I need to get out of here." But she didn't move. They
were alone in the library of Xavier Franklin's mansion
with a party going on outside the heavy closed doors. She
could hear it—the voices, the laughter, the band playing
some up-tempo but classical number.

"So despite you telling me a minute ago that you're
indifferent to me," Ryan said, "what you're now saying
is that you hate me."

She nodded. "I can't stand you."

"But you still want to kiss me."

Yes. She needed to kiss him, to do more than just kiss
him. To feel Ryan's hands on her, his hot skin beneath
her fingertips. To feel him sliding inside of her, filling
her the way she'd always fantasized about. Even in the

months that he'd been out of her life, she'd still dreamed about having him in her bed.

Damn.

It was Emma who closed the distance between them first. Her mind was foggy, but her body knew what it wanted. It wanted Ryan. It had always wanted Ryan since the moment she'd met him. And the Desidero potion, just a small splash of it, had heightened that need inside of her to an uncontrollable level.

Just because it was inconvenient didn't mean it wasn't true.

Ryan looked concerned. "Emma, we need to—"

"Shut up." She took his face between her hands to pull him closer and crushed her mouth against his.

3

EMMA BLACK, a woman who proclaimed to hate his guts, was kissing him more passionately than he'd ever been kissed. He could feel her desire like it was a palpable thing. It sank into him, making his cock harder than it had ever been a day in his life.

Ryan filled his hands with her thick, silky red hair, letting it slide through his fingers. Her grip tightened on him, pulling him even closer to her.

He'd wanted her from the moment he'd seen her in the middle of the party earlier, rescuing him from some random socialite who'd wanted to get into his pants. His desire for Emma had been immediate—at least, after he'd gotten over his initial shock at seeing her again after all this time. The potion simply took that desire and increased it to a level that was impossible to ignore.

He'd sought her out, hoping to talk to her, to tell her the truth—that he'd been set up, that he wasn't a thief and had been wrongfully fired—and see if that made any difference to her. See if she believed him.

He'd wanted her to believe him.

When he'd seen that horny old bastard pawing her, his blood began to boil. If Franklin had been thirty years younger, he might have received more than a glare and a lie about being Emma's fiancé.

"You taste like champagne," he whispered against her lips when she pulled back an inch, her breath coming fast and deep.

"I had a glass earlier."

"You taste so good."

"So do you."

Emma slid her hands down the front of his shirt, over his chest to his abdomen. Her touch felt like fire. He saw the same aching desire he felt reflected in her eyes.

Proof.

The proof he needed that she didn't hate him. This was it.

Franklin said the potion didn't work for him. Likely he'd tried it on many women, hoping they'd throw themselves into his arms and bed. Dirty old man.

But the Desidero potion didn't work like that.

It didn't make Guinevere desire King Arthur. Instead, she fell hard for Lancelot. It meant that she'd wanted the knight over the king all along, but had resisted due to her situation.

Once the potion worked its special magic, she'd had no choice but to give in to her true desires. The potion simply acted as a push against any control its victim might have.

If Emma had truly hated Ryan—or even if she'd been indifferent to him as she claimed—the potion wouldn't work at all.

Emma wanted him as Guinevere had wanted Lancelot.

And King Arthur had been sent packing.

"Do you feel it?" he asked.

"Feel it?" She slid her hand down over the front of

his pants where his erection strained and she grinned wickedly at him. "I think so."

He groaned and swore darkly under his breath. "That's not exactly what I meant."

"Yes, I feel the potion's effects. No doubt about it."

"You want me."

She brushed her lips over his throat. "I hate you."

He couldn't help but smile at the obvious lie. She didn't hate him. She might wish she did, but she didn't. "So you *don't* want me."

She took his face between her hands and stared deeply into his eyes. "What I want is to feel you inside of me."

He inhaled sharply as she slid her hand down over his cock again. "You have a definite way with words, Em."

"I've been told that before."

Any amusement on his part disappeared as she unzipped him with deft hands and reached inside his fly to wrap her fingers around his hard length. He groaned.

"Sit down." She pushed him backward until he bumped into the couch behind him. He sat down hard.

"If you insist." He reached for her, wanting to pull the straps of her dress down over her shoulders and bare her breasts to his touch, his mouth, but she slipped out of his reach, instead sinking down to the floor in front of him.

He eyed the closed but not locked door. "Emma…we should leave, go somewhere else—somewhere private. We shouldn't do this here—"

But he couldn't speak any more when she took him into her mouth. He arched his back, the intense pleasure crashing over him, almost too much to bear. He had to struggle to find some semblance of control or he feared he would explode right then and there. His hands shook as he pushed the vibrant red hair off her forehead so he could see her face, watch her lush, pink lips slide down onto him. Her mouth was so hot and wet—he couldn't speak, couldn't think…he could only feel…

Finally, he was able to gather himself enough to moan her name. "Emma…*please*…" He pulled at her and suddenly her lips were on his again, hard and hot, devouring him with the kiss that held so much passion it was as if she were starving. She crawled onto his lap to straddle him.

His hands sought her full breasts, squeezing them through the top of her dress and running his hands down her sides, over her ass, fingers digging into the soft flesh, and slipping under her skirt toward her sex. She wore panties, but they were a very flimsy barrier. Pushing them to the side, he was able to slide his fingers against the slickness of her, which earned him a shuddery breath and a moan of encouragement.

Ryan shifted a little, replacing his fingers with the head of his cock which he rubbed against her. She was so wet for him, so ready. He had to be inside of her. He would go insane if he didn't take her here, now. He'd never wanted anyone as much as this. The potion had made it impossible to deny what he'd always wanted.

Emma.

"Yes," she moaned. "Please, Ryan…"

"You want me."

"Yes."

"Even though you think you hate me."

"Yes!"

When he was perfectly positioned to enter her with one upward thrust, he heard the sound.

Knocking.

"Is somebody in there?" the voice asked from the other side of the door.

Then there was the sound of the knob turning.

The very next moment, Emma had pulled away from him, scrambling back as if she'd just been hit in the face with a glass of ice cold water. She stared at him with eyes as wide as saucers and hurriedly pulled the straps of her dress back up into place.

"This was a horrible mistake," she said, finally averting her eyes.

Then she was gone, grabbing her purse and scurrying out of the room as if the fire alarm had gone off. She passed a couple at the door who wore matching purple masks. Ryan had the chance to tuck himself away and zip up before their attention moved to him.

"Did we interrupt something?" the man asked.

"Yes," he growled, when what he really wanted to do was get up and throttle the both of them.

They looked at each other before closing the door behind them, leaving him in the library alone.

His first inclination was to chase after Emma and talk to her. To finish what they'd started. But he knew it was too late for that tonight. She'd found a fraction of control again, despite the potion's effects.

From what he could remember about the Desidero potion, those effects would fade over time. A week at the most.

Being apart would help, but not much. His body craved her now—and he knew the feeling was mutual. If they consummated their desire, the potion's effects would fade quickly—a day at the most. If they didn't—it might be a difficult week ahead if he wanted to think about anything but Emma's touch, her mouth, her tongue, her body…

Torture.

His gaze moved to the side table where the green

bottle sat innocently and then he looked down at the floor where Emma had left behind a black tote bag.

Cinderella had left the ball and forgotten a couple items, though neither was your typical glass slipper. He was no Prince Charming, but it seemed like a fitting fairy tale at the moment.

She probably believed that she'd escaped just in time and that everything would be okay now. That she'd never see Ryan Shephard again, accused thief and liar, a man she swore she hated.

Only her desire and out of control lust for Ryan wouldn't just vanish into thin air. And there wasn't anything she could do about that, other than try to avoid him.

Emma Black desired him. The potion proved that once and for all. He knew she'd been fond of him when they were partners, but this? This was more than he could have imagined.

And she'd been the aggressor, practically throwing him on the sofa so she could have her way with him.

The thought brought a slow smile to his face.

He grabbed the tote bag and unzipped it to see what was inside. Books—about a dozen trade paperbacks, all identical. He pulled one out and looked at the cover.

INEVITABLE
E.M. Black

There was the shadowy outline of a female's naked back and buttocks to the side of the dust jacket. A male figure stood behind her, his hand curling around from behind to rest on the small of her spine. It was subtle, but there was no doubt this was supposed to be a sexy book.

Ryan couldn't help but grin. "My goodness, Emma, you naughty girl. What are you reading these days?"

He turned it over to read the story blurb on the back cover. It was about a woman who worked for a paranormal investigation agency who experienced many explicit fantasies made flesh during her cases with her partner Bryan.

Bryan.

Ryan frowned and flipped through the book to find the bio of the author. There was a black-and-white picture, but it was mysteriously shot so it wasn't obvious what she really looked like. Her back was to the camera, her face turned just a little so she was coyly glancing over her shoulder. Very enigmatic. Very sexy.

Very Emma.

He recognized her immediately and his mouth fell open in shock.

There was a card clipped to one of the book covers and he grabbed it.

Emma, congrats on the new release. Enjoy the extra copies! Please consider writing more for me. Let me know when you're ready to talk more books!
—Marilyn

Emma wrote this book. She was E.M. Black. These were copies of her erotic novel.

Naughty, indeed.

He sat down heavily on the leather sofa and trained his gaze on the door, waiting for Emma to come bursting through at any moment to reclaim her tote bag and potion bottle.

She didn't return.

Ryan left the party at just after eleven o'clock and

grabbed a taxi to take him across the city to his hotel room. He hadn't spoken to Franklin personally about who was supplying him with stolen supernatural merchandise. This was still vitally important to him—to clear his name once and for all—but he'd decided to put that on hold for just a couple days longer.

Tomorrow he'd rent a car and head to Mystic Ridge, a town he hadn't stepped foot in since he'd been fired six months ago.

He had to see Emma again.

Tonight, however, he had some serious reading to do.

4

EMMA WAS ON THE BUS headed away from the station when she realized, with a sick, sinking feeling, that she'd left a couple of things behind.

The books she could live without. Since she'd left them in a library, maybe Xavier would think they were an anonymous donation. He certainly seemed the type to appreciate erotica. But the bottle—that was going to be a problem. It was, after all, the sole reason she'd been sent to see the billionaire in the first place.

Of course, that was before everything went to hell.

Her head still felt cloudy and she couldn't believe what she'd done. She and Ryan had almost—

She banged her head gently against the window, feeling the vibrations of the bus's movement.

It was as if her baser instincts had taken over. She'd jumped on the man she claimed to hate like a sex-starved frog on a tuxedo-wearing lily pad.

In her line of work, she'd come into contact with potions before, but she'd never been influenced by one. Not like this. It was just a good thing that she wouldn't see Ryan again. Ever. She definitely didn't want a repeat performance to mess her head up even more than it already was.

The window reflected a redhead who had sad, glossy eyes and flushed cheeks. Emma shook a finger at her. "Don't get emotional over that jerk."

The redhead just stared back at her bleakly.

"No," she assured her reflection. "He's bad news. Not worth another thought."

The lust potion had brought back a big mess of issues, all of them involving her unrequited feelings for Ryan. The ones that would have to stay unrequited.

She didn't trust him. He was a thief and a liar.

For a moment she thought he was going to try to tell her that he was innocent, that he'd been wrongfully fired from his job. He'd seemed surprised when she told him there'd been a witness to what he'd done, one Emma trusted more than anyone.

Herself.

Emma had seen Ryan leave the office with the stolen merchandise in hand late one night. She'd been in the parking lot. She'd seen him load the stolen items in the trunk of a black car and then take off without looking back.

If she hadn't seen it with her own eyes, she never would have believed it. But she had. And she did. And the fact that she still had feelings for the man who'd broken her trust as well as her heart—well, that just pissed her off.

Thank God she'd stopped before they'd had sex. It had been so close. Way too close. She squeezed her eyes shut and tried not to think about how he'd felt, how he'd tasted, how he'd smelled. Very good. Very tempting. Very dangerous.

"Goodbye, Ryan," she whispered. "For good this time."

"OKAY, WELL PLEASE contact me if you find anything," Emma said into the phone Thursday afternoon. She was finally back at her desk at the PARA head office. She'd taken the morning off since her bus hadn't pulled into Mystic Ridge until after 2:00 a.m. "I really appreciate it."

She slammed the receiver down and then swore at it.

Her friend, Charlotte Hayes, eyed her cautiously. "And what did that poor phone ever do to you?"

"They can't find the potion bottle," Emma explained. "That was one of the maids. They're still cleaning up after the party last night. No bottle. No tote bag. Nothing."

"That blows."

"Tell me about it."

"It's not the end of the world. It happens. Jeez, Emma, old man Franklin hitting on you must have really messed up your head. You never forget stuff like this."

Emma cringed. It was a pretty good excuse, she thought. She'd left the party after Xavier had groped her. That was all she'd told Charlotte. She hadn't made one mention about seeing Ryan again. After all, it had been statuesque, blonde and beautiful Charlotte whom he'd dated before he was fired. And it had been Charlotte whom Emma had been painfully envious of for that very reason. However, Charlotte had gotten over Ryan's betrayal much faster than Emma had.

The last thing she wanted Charlotte to know was that Emma had bumped into her former partner and had nearly screwed his brains out at a client's home, thanks to a lust potion.

Talk about unprofessional. And embarrassing.

It was best she forget about it. She was still working on that.

It wasn't as if she resented Charlotte for being tall and gorgeous. She liked her. A lot. In fact, they'd been roommates until only until a few months ago. Charlotte had worked for PARA a year now. She was only twenty-five. Her parents had money, a lot of it, but most of it had been lost in a bad economy and a Ponzi scheme, leaving Charlotte with no nest egg to speak of. She'd had to get a job to pay her bills instead of relying on Mom and Dad, so she'd jumped at the chance to make a living using her empathic ability.

The poor girl still didn't know the value of a dollar. Emma had taken her under her wing and shown her the ropes of bargain hunting. Or she'd tried to, anyway. When you were born into money, it was difficult to make the transition to clipping coupons.

At least she was gorgeous. And she was dating a man who was crazy about her. Charlotte and Stephen had recently moved in together, actually. She'd be fine. Emma just worried about the people she cared about.

Charlotte had been put in charge of sorting through unsolved cases and she had a stack of file folders on her desk. Emma had glanced through them earlier. One was a known thorn in PARA's side, an allegedly haunted hotel on the other side of Mystic Ridge. For years, agents had been unsuccessful at exorcising the ghost from the location—even proving there was even a ghost in residence seemed impossible.

If Emma messed up on any more assignments, she'd be demoted into working side by side with Charlotte on those cold cases. She wasn't quite as fond of dusty and impossible-to-solve riddles as Charlotte seemed to be.

Agency manager Patrick McKay moved slowly toward her. Tall and attractive with a bright gold wedding ring on his left hand to show he'd recently returned from his honeymoon, he used a cane to walk these days as part of his recovery from a spinal injury. Otherwise he looked like someone who might climb mountains in his spare time.

"Any luck locating the bottle, Emma?" he asked.

She just shook her head, trying to ignore her feelings of guilt over her failure.

His lips thinned and his gaze grew concerned. "Everything okay, Emma? It's not like you to forget something so important."

"I'm fine. And I— I'm sorry, Patrick. I don't know what happened."

"Xavier Franklin hit on her and it messed her up," Charlotte offered bluntly. "She shouldn't have been sent to that dirty old man's home all by herself. She's lucky she got out of there at all."

Patrick's brows drew together. "Is that true?"

Emma tensed. "Yes, but I don't want to make a big deal over it."

"Franklin is a known womanizer, but I hoped his age might prohibit him from bothering my agents. Seems like I was wrong. I'm sorry you had to deal with that. And Charlotte's right. You need a partner to prevent situations like this happening in the future. You'll be able to do more field assignments than you have the last few months. I'm sure you're sick of being stuck at your desk so much lately."

"But—"

He raised an eyebrow. "Yes?"

Her shoulders sank. "That's fine. Thanks."

He watched her for a moment. "You're sure everything's fine, Emma? I sense that you're troubled."

Empaths. They were dangerous to be around. Especially really gifted ones like Patrick.

"I'm fine," she said firmly.

"If you say so."

"I do."

She was. She was fine. And she held on to that thought for the rest of the day until it was time to go home. She had a date tonight and the least she could do would be to show up for it even though all she really wanted to do was go home and crawl into her bed.

But forgetting that potion bottle was unforgivable and unprofessional. It bothered her.

Emma exited the PARA head office and headed toward her car in the parking lot—a blue Toyota Camry that had been in the shop yesterday, which was why she'd had to take the bus to New York. She pushed her key into the lock, but then stopped. A shiver went through her and gathered low in her body. Her nipples tightened and strained against her white shirt.

She bit her bottom lip. *Uh, oh.*

Her cell phone vibrated. She grabbed for it and held it to her ear. "Yes?"

"Miss me?"

Her jaw clenched. "Ryan."

"You recognize my voice."

"Where are you? I know you're here."

"How do you know that?"

"I can *feel* you."

"I'm flattered."

"Where are you right now?"

"Behind you."

She looked over her shoulder to see him leaning against a nearby car and her grip tightened on the phone. He removed his phone from his ear and tucked it into the pocket of his leather jacket.

"I just wanted to talk to you," he said.

She pressed the Disconnect button on her phone and tossed it into her purse. Lust potions were very powerful, in case she had any question about that. She was the living proof that being within twenty feet of Ryan made her desperate for him.

She eyed him wearily. "Just leave me alone, Ryan. I have a date tonight and it's definitely not with you."

His gaze remained fixed on her. "I dreamed about you last night."

"Good dream or bad?"

"Very good." There was a dozen feet between them and yet it felt as if he was right next to her. He rubbed his temples and looked pained for a moment. "This is more difficult than I thought it would be. Being this close to you feels…dangerous."

"I might not like you, but I know you won't hurt me."

"Who said *you* were the one in danger?" He grinned a little.

She glanced around. "You really need to go, Ryan. If anyone sees you…"

"They'll firmly escort me off the premises?"

"If you're lucky."

"I just wanted to see you again. I…*needed* to see you again."

The desperate tone in his voice gave her an unexpected inner thrill. "Why?"

"Because I wanted to give you something."

He drew closer. She found that she wasn't scurrying back into the office like she probably should. Instead she pressed back against her car door as he came within a couple of feet from her. Her heart rate increased and her skin warmed.

She watched him carefully. From the heated look in his gaze to the sight of his chest moving with rapid breathing, it was obvious she affected him as much as he affected her.

Dangerous indeed.

He reached for her hand, taking it in his. The contact left her breathless. The potion's effects hadn't faded a bit from yesterday. If anything, this strong lust she felt for her former partner had gotten stronger. He moved closer still. She was certain he was going to kiss her, to press his mouth against hers. And she was going to let him do more than that.

"What do you want to give me?" she whispered, when his lips were only an inch away from hers. She braced her right hand against his firm chest so she could feel the pounding of his heart.

"You forgot something last night."

She felt a press of something cold and hard in the palm of her left hand and she looked down to see the green potion bottle.

He'd come all the way back to Mystic Ridge to return the bottle of Desidero potion to her.

"Ryan…" she whispered, not sure if she was going to thank him or ask why he'd bothered.

"Later, Em." He turned and walked away. The moment he was out of view, she leaned against her car door, the only thing currently keeping her vertical. Every cell in her body had urged her to throw her arms around him, kiss him, undress him. It didn't matter that they were right in the middle of the PARA employee parking lot. Her body burned for him to be inside of her.

It was *very* inconvenient.

And she had a funny feeling that she hadn't seen the last of him.

IT WOULD HAVE BEEN MUCH simpler for Ryan to leave the bottle on Emma's doorstep so she could find it, take it back to PARA and say her assignment was completed successfully. It hadn't been necessary for him to deliver it in person, he thought.

What had started off as a bit of a joke, a small amusement for him after so many months of being alone, had gotten serious damn fast. As much as he wanted Emma, she simply wasn't in his grand plan. Every minute he spent here in Mystic Ridge was one less minute he'd spend investigating who was really behind the crimes of which he'd been accused. He had a list of stolen items he'd been tracking. Six in total. He'd found only two of them so far—an enchanted amulet and an urn—in the collections of rich men with too much time and money on their side.

He was certain Xavier Franklin, a known collector of glassware, was in possession of a missing vase, but hadn't been able to officially confirm that at the party. He'd have to go back and question the billionaire as soon as he could.

Ryan's confidence in his plan had faded with each month that passed. It seemed as if everyone had moved on except him.

He wondered sometimes why he refused to give up. Why not just head down to Florida early? Down there he could start over. He'd make new friends, find a beautiful woman who could look at him without doubt or disappointment in her eyes, and make a new life for himself once and for all.

Yes, that's exactly what he was going to do.

But not just yet.

First he had clear his name. It was the principle of the thing.

He didn't even really fault Emma's immediate assumption that he was guilty. It wasn't common knowledge, but Ryan did have a bit of a shady history. Fifteen years ago, he'd fallen in with his brother's friends, a tough group of kids who jacked cars and sold the parts. Ryan was one of the unlucky ones who'd been busted for it.

The cop who'd nabbed him took pity on a seventeen-year-old kid who was missing the right direction in his life and helped to keep him out of jail, helped him see that the path he was on was one that would only lead to more trouble. Ryan hadn't stolen anything since. He'd learned his lesson. But those he'd trusted and told about his past would know that his being light-fingered was a definite possibility.

He stayed in touch with the cop for years. The man had been like a father to him in his late teens and early twenties and had helped keep Ryan on the straight and narrow. It had a whole lot to do with the man's influence that Ryan was going this extra mile to clear his name.

He missed the old guy. In fact, Ryan still visited his grave every other weekend.

But it hadn't made anything easier over the last six months, knowing right from wrong.

It had even occurred to him a couple of times that he should live up to his reputation and start to steal again. If he was considered a thief by everyone, he may as well make a profit at it.

But it just wasn't in his nature anymore.

It wasn't in his brother's nature anymore either. Joe had cleaned up years ago and started the business down south. He was the one who'd asked Ryan for help, knowing Ryan's gift with cars.

So Ryan endeavored to prove his innocence, to make that cop who'd been his one good influence in his youth proud, even beyond the grave. But he kept coming up against brick walls every direction he turned.

"Brick walls are a hell of a lot better than jail cells," he mumbled as he drove his Mustang away from just down the block from where he'd left Emma.

Ryan wanted to get back to working at clearing his name as soon as possible, but he wasn't quite ready to say goodbye to his favorite stubborn redhead just yet. They had some unfinished business between them to take care of first.

5

TALL, DARK AND HANDSOME. Yes, Leo Barker was definitely all that.

Emma gazed past her glass of red wine and across the table at her date. Leo was new in town. Thirty-two, gorgeous, a local orthodontist. He drove a Mercedes. If Mystic Ridge had a list of eligible bachelors, there was no doubt Leo would be right at the top.

They'd met last week at the grocery store when their carts had collided.

A total small-town love story in the making, she thought.

They were having dinner at a small but elegant Italian restaurant, newly opened in a converted Victorian house. It held fifteen tables at the most in a dimly lit dining area, red tablecloths and candles decorating each table. There was even violin music. It was all very romantic.

Even though Emma was dealing with the affects of a potion that made her desperately lust after another man whenever he was close by, she really didn't see any reason why she should cancel the date. After her confrontation with Ryan, she quickly delivered the bottle of Desidero potion to the PARA potions department, and then rushed home to get ready—hair, make-up, the works. She picked out a low-cut teal blouse that made her hair look even more vibrantly red, and a black pencil skirt that helped her legs look just a bit longer. Black stilettos, no hose. She was good to go.

When she'd left the house with Leo, she could have sworn she'd seen Ryan again out of the corner of her eye. Only more proof he was haunting her.

Now that she was in the middle of the date—despite the care she'd taken in trying to look as good as possible—she knew she wasn't putting her best effort forward. Every time she closed her eyes she saw Ryan's face.

It was annoying as hell.

"Having a good time?" Leo asked.

She opened her eyes. "Fantastic."

"More wine?"

She put her hand over her glass. "No, thanks. I think I've already drank most of that bottle."

"I'm driving, so it doesn't matter."

"I don't think you want to deal with a drunk woman tonight."

"Let me be the judge of that." He smiled and every one of his teeth were like perfect little white rectangles. Flawless. She cocked her head to the side.

"Your teeth are perfect," she said, then pressed her lips together. She'd already had too much wine. She was speaking her thoughts aloud without much of a filter. It was more of a sign to shut things down as far as alcohol was concerned.

Not that she was worried about sleeping with Leo on their first date. He was gorgeous and available, but the last thing she wanted to do was have sex with one man while fantasizing about another.

Besides, now that she wasn't anywhere close to Ryan,

she felt totally in control of herself. No tingles. No uncontrollable desire. Nothing. Which led her to believe that despite Leo's good looks and nice résumé, she just wasn't attracted to him. It happened. It was disappointing, but it happened.

Just like King Arthur and Guinevere.

She grimaced at the thought.

"They're porcelain," Leo said.

She blinked at him. "Excuse me?"

"My teeth. You commented on how perfect they are."

"Oh, right. Yes. Sorry."

He nodded. "They *are* perfect, thank you for noticing. Your teeth are lovely, but if you want to go that extra step and make them perfect as well, then I could certainly help you out. It's a very simple process actually and I've never had a client who's regretted their decision to get veneers."

Now she felt self-conscious about her slightly less than perfect teeth. "I'll definitely keep that in mind."

"If you'll excuse me for a moment." He stood up from the table. "While I'm gone, why don't you decide what you'd like for dessert?"

"Dessert?"

"Yes, of course. Got to finish dinner with something sweet. Just make sure to brush and floss afterward." He winked at her.

She forced a smile. "Of course."

He left the table and she pressed back in her seat, closing her eyes. There was Ryan again, right on the other side of her eyelids. She didn't particularly like that she was compelled to do this frequently, but just thinking about him made her feel better. In her imagination, he had the exact opposite effect he had on her when he was there in person. In person he excited her and drove her crazy—just like he'd always done. In her imagination he calmed her and made her wish things could be different.

This time imagining Ryan did brush a flush to her skin and a pleasant shiver ran down her body and slid between her legs. The desire that had been lacking while speaking with Leo had suddenly returned in full force.

Which meant only one thing.

She forced herself to open her eyes.

Ryan now sat across from her.

"Evening, Em," he said.

She gripped the edge of the table. "Why are you here?"

"I was out for a walk and saw you through the window."

Her eyes narrowed. "You're lying. I thought I saw you by my house earlier. You followed me here, didn't you?"

He shrugged. "Think what you like. I'll keep my secrets."

"Are you trying to ruin my evening?"

"That's not my intention. Really."

He looked particularly delicious tonight in a blue button-down shirt the same vivid color of his eyes. It was tight enough that it showed his broad shoulders off to their best advantage.

She snapped her eyes back up to his face. "Go away."

"Does your date know about us?"

She just looked at him. "Us?"

"About our situation."

She sighed. "Ryan, why are tormenting me?"

"Tormenting you. That doesn't sound the least bit sexy,

does it? And yet it feels so good." He reached across the table to touch her hand. The contact sent a bolt of desire directly to her groin and she snatched her hand back.

Emma wagged a finger at him. "Don't do that."

"So strict."

She glanced over her shoulder at the restrooms. "My date will be back any minute."

"Then I suppose I should speed this along."

"What?"

She heard the sound of something heavy hitting the table. She turned back around and her gaze closed on the object. It was a copy of *Inevitable*. Her eyes shot to Ryan and widened.

"You left this behind along with the bottle," he said casually. "I've got the rest of them in my car."

She grimaced, but decided to play it cool. She waited until the waiter walked past carrying two plates of Fettuccini Alfredo toward a neighboring table before she answered. "Okay, you caught me. I like to read sexy books every now and then. Big deal. I'm not embarrassed."

"You're the author."

She felt herself pale. She wanted to keep her writing a secret. The last person she'd want to know about it was Ryan. "Am not."

The denial sounded weak, even to her own ears.

"Don't even attempt to deny it, Em. The picture is of you. The name isn't even that much different from your regular name. If you're trying to stay incognito, it's not working very well. I think a little part of you wants to be exposed." He raised an eyebrow. "In more ways than one."

She willed away the sudden panicky feeling she got in her gut. This was not the worst thing to happen. If people found out about her publishing career, it wouldn't be the end of the world.

Emma exhaled slowly and eyed the violin player as he slowly passed their table. The buzz of other diners' conversations made it difficult to concentrate. "Big deal, Ryan. I wrote a sexy book in my spare time. And I'm damn good at it."

"I'll say."

Again he surprised her. "Excuse me?"

"You're a good writer."

"You read it?"

"Oh, yes." He grabbed the book and thumbed through it. "I even dog-eared the pages I liked best."

"Then consider that your copy." She forced a smile and hoped that her cheeks didn't appear as flushed as they felt. "My gift to you. Would you like it signed?"

"Absolutely." He smiled and his blue eyes locked with hers. "Interesting that the hero is named Bryan."

Her heart started pounding faster. "It's a common name."

"And he's also the heroine's business partner. And they investigate paranormal phenomena."

"So?"

He leaned back. "I guess you're going to pretend that Bryan isn't based on me."

"He isn't."

"Looks like me, sounds like me, same role in your life—"

"You're not my partner anymore."

"—and your heroine, who frankly sounds a whole lot like you, can't keep her hands off of him. Really, Em, I had no idea what a dirty little mind you have. A couple scenes in here even made me blush. They're the scenes I dog-eared so I can read them again later."

She glared at him. "Do you have a purpose for barging into the middle of my date or was it just to embarrass me?"

"Is there another option?"

"No."

"Listen, what I want is a chance to talk to you. Just you and me without any negativity swirling around. Do you think that's possible?"

"If you wanted that, then you shouldn't have waved this book in my face and tried to make me feel self-conscious about it."

Ryan looked a bit confused. "Why would you feel self-conscious? Em, you have to own what you like to do and to hell with anyone else's opinion. It's a great book. Quite honestly, I was going to tease you about it a bit, but then I read it and...I liked it."

She studied him to see if he was lying to her. It was hard to tell with Ryan. Her face warmed at the unexpected compliment. "You should join my Facebook page."

"Maybe I will. Now that I know your secret identity."

"It doesn't matter anyway. This is the only one I'll be writing."

He frowned. "Why?"

"I want to focus on my career with PARA."

"I don't see why you can't do both. I think it would be a mistake for you to stop doing something you're so good at." The gazes locked and a warm emotion that went well beyond lust slid behind his blue eyes. "Hell, Em. You still don't know how amazing you are, do you?"

How she wanted him. Right here. Right now. Her body ached for his, every minute he was close to her. And it was moments like this that Emma remembered why she'd begun to fall for him before. Why she still cared about him even after everything that had happened. He could tease and turn on the charm when it suited him, but underneath that shiny layer was something else, something vulnerable that he'd allowed her to see when they'd been friends and partners. It was something she liked, was drawn to, and wanted to see more of. But he seemed hesitant to let that glossy exterior slip very often.

She knew Charlotte had never seen that deeper side of Ryan. She'd been so happy with the exterior package, she didn't bother to look too deeply inside.

At this point, Emma was afraid what more she might find if she looked too closely and how much she'd like it.

She knew Ryan had had a troubled youth that got him in hot water with the police. He'd confided this to her once when they'd been staked out in a car for six hours.

Damn. If she hadn't seen him steal with her own eyes, she never would have believed it. But it had happened. And the fact that he'd denied it to her face kept her from ever entertaining the possibility of something more with him.

She could deal with a repentant criminal who wanted to change his ways, but a bold-faced liar was not someone she wanted in her life. Her father had been like that. His abandonment still crushed her. She didn't want a repeat performance from another man she willingly gave her love and trust to.

Maybe it was already too late. Maybe that was exactly why she'd been so heartbroken by his betrayal. Maybe she hadn't just been falling for him—she'd already fallen.

Leo approached the table and paused when he saw Ryan. He stretched out his hand.

"Leo Barker," he said. "And you are?"

"Ryan Shephard." Ryan shook his hand. "A friend of Emma's. A very *good* friend."

"Not anymore," Emma said tightly. "I believe I asked you to leave."

"Oh, come on, Em, don't be like that."

She was feeling a multitude of emotions at the moment. A high level of exasperation, a lot of embarrassment, and there was still the unbidden desire that swirled within her being so near to Ryan. She'd never wanted to throttle someone and tear his clothes off and have sex with him at the same time. It was a strange combination.

And damn if she didn't find him amusing as well. Only Ryan would stroll in here, in the middle of her date, and claim that the character in her erotic novel was based on him.

She'd feel much more freedom to laugh it off if it wasn't one hundred percent true.

Leo frowned. "Emma, are you saying that you asked him to leave and he didn't?"

"Yes," she confirmed.

"Is this an ex of yours?"

"You could say that," Emma said. "But not the way you think."

Ryan didn't budge from his seat. "Emma and I have history. A lot of history. There was a time when we would practically finish each other's sentences, we were that close. A relationship like that doesn't just dissolve because of a few unfortunate misunderstandings."

Emma rolled her eyes. "We were only partners for a year. Let's not get carried away."

"No, *let's*." Ryan grinned. "Look, Leo, no offense. You seem like a stand-up sort of fellow. But you're just not Emma's type."

"Oh?" Leo eyed him. "And what is Emma's type?"

"Me," he said bluntly.

She just stared across the table at him, temporarily speechless.

"Is that right?" Leo retorted. "Then it's odd that she's out for dinner with me tonight and not you, isn't it?"

"Well, right now she thinks she hates me, but she doesn't. I've come back to town to see if I can prove that. She doesn't think she wants me here, but she really does. She just has to realize that."

"I see," Leo said. "Pardon me for saying this, but that sounds like something a stalker would say. Someone who refuses to take no for an answer."

There wasn't even a fraction of friendliness in his tone. Ryan gave him a stunned look.

"A stalker?" There was now an edge of anger to Ryan's voice. "You obviously don't know me because I'd never harm a hair on Emma's head."

"Then prove that and leave. You're clearly not wanted here."

Ryan stood up and glared at him. "You think so, huh?"

"Yeah, I do."

Emma sighed. "Ryan, seriously. You need to go now."

He looked at her and frowned. Disappointment slid behind his gaze. "Fine. If that's what you want. But I will see you later."

There was a woman standing right behind him. He turned to leave and Emma gasped as he slammed right into her.

But, wait. He didn't slam into her. He walked right through her as if he hadn't even seen her. As if she wasn't even there.

Ryan turned at the sound of Emma's gasp. "What's wrong?"

She took a deep breath and let it out slowly. "I think she wants to tell us something."

"Who?"

"The ghost," she said. "You're standing right next to her."

6

THE GHOST, A PRETTY BLONDE woman who wore a blue dress with thick straps and a full skirt, her hair in a tight chignon, turned to Emma. "You can see me?"

She nodded. "I can."

The woman's gaze moved toward Leo and Ryan. "And these men are arguing over you?"

Emma grimaced. "Seem to be."

Ryan broke away from Leo and glared at him, before turning to Emma. "There's a ghost here?"

Leo looked around. "What are you talking about?"

"I know the hotel close by is allegedly haunted, but I didn't know about this location." She looked at the woman. "Considering how many clairvoyants this town has in it, that surprises me."

"This restaurant only opened a few weeks ago," the woman explained, patting her hair absently as if to keep it perfectly in place. "Before that, it was my home, unoccupied for years and years."

The woman looked upset. Her eyes were shiny with silvery tears, and her voice cracked on her words.

"Are you all right?" Emma asked. It seemed a strange question to ask a dead person, but from her experience, they liked to be treated just like everybody else whenever possible.

The woman nodded. "It's my anniversary. I miss my husband so much that I wanted to try to see him, but I can't. I never can. I'm stuck here just as I always have been."

Emma glanced around at the dining room. Everyone had stopped eating and were staring at her with varying degrees of disbelief and shock on their faces. Just because the town boasted a paranormal investigation agency in a shiny glass building downtown, didn't mean that everyone believed in ghosts. Most of them would simply see a woman talking to herself.

She knew Ryan had drawn closer because a shiver of desire slid through her that only increased when he pressed his hand to the small of her back.

"Maybe we should take this discussion somewhere a bit more private," he suggested.

"Good idea," she agreed.

"Excuse me?" Leo said. "I believe we were in the middle of our date before we were rudely interrupted."

"You're right. I'm so sorry." She approached him and looked up at his incredulous expression. He wasn't a bad guy. He didn't deserve any of this. She wondered if the date would have gone better if Ryan hadn't been a problem at the moment for her. She'd have to bet on... *maybe*.

Just maybe.

"Maybe we can try again another night," she said. "Is that possible?"

He frowned before his expression relaxed a little. He flicked an unfriendly look at Ryan and then back at her. "I think that's possible."

"Thank you." She went to give him a quick kiss on

his cheek, but he turned his mouth to hers and kissed her fully on her lips. He tasted minty, as if he'd just brushed his teeth during his trip to the restroom. She had no doubt that was exactly what he'd done. He deepened the kiss, pulling her against him like some hero in a romance novel and she braced her hands against his chest. Finally she broke away and drew in a shaky breath.

Then Leo looked directly at Ryan and smirked, which totally ruined it for her. The kiss had only been to show up the man Leo perceived as competition.

Not sexy.

Ryan just watched them, his arms crossed in front of him. "Fantastic," he said dryly. "I'll give it a ten out of ten. Done now?"

"For now," Leo replied.

"We have ghost business and you're just a civilian. So, buh-bye."

Leo looked at her. "I can wait and drive you home."

Emma shook her head. "It's all right. I'll be fine."

"I'll call you."

"Okay. Thanks."

Leo threw some money on the table and with a last glare sent in Ryan's direction, he walked out of the restaurant.

The ghost had watched this exchange with growing interest. "You seem to be very popular."

Emma looked at her. "I peaked late."

The ghost pursed her lips. "The man who just left seems to be the better choice for you. This one," she eyed Ryan, "looks like trouble."

"Tell me about it."

"And yet you desire him more."

Emma cringed. "Is it that obvious?"

"To me it is."

Ghosts were typically extremely intuitive. Something about being dead gave them special insight into the hearts of humans.

Leaving the dining room and the curious onlookers hanging on every word they spoke—apart from the ghost that none of them could see or hear except for Emma—they walked out toward the front doors. Emma tried desperately to focus on business rather than the close proximity of Ryan's warm body to hers.

"Can you leave this building?" Emma asked.

"I can go outside, but I can only stray ten feet from the property. That's it."

The home the restaurant was housed in had been around for more than a hundred years. The dress the ghost was wearing, though, placed her in the forties. That would have been when she'd died.

Ryan opened the front door for Emma to exit through. During their few months as partners, he knew what to do when they were on a case involving ghosts. He'd stand back, keep watch, make sure nothing went wrong as Emma communicated with the spirit. A lot of ghosts weren't all that open to conversations, but if they were, a lot of information could be gathered. Usually the point was to convince the spirit that they were dead, that it was time for them to move on. And that bright light they sometimes saw out of their peripheral vision was something they wanted to head toward in order to move on to the next plane of existence.

It wasn't a difficult process, but sometimes it got a bit tricky.

Like when the ghost refused to leave. Sometimes the ghost decided to be a nuisance at best and a danger at worst to the living people inhabiting the haunted location. That was usually when an exorcism needed to be done.

"You said it's your anniversary," Emma said.

"Yes."

"What's your name?"

The ghost hesitated. "Lorraine."

"Lorraine...last name?"

"Duchamp."

The name seemed familiar to Emma. "Do you know what year this is?"

"Yes, of course. I know I've been dead a very long time and I know that I'm a ghost."

"Good to hear. So what's the problem?"

"The problem?" She sighed and it sounded weary. "The problem is that my husband is a fool."

"How so?"

"Do you see that building over there..." She gazed off into the darkness and Emma followed her line of sight toward a five-storey hotel which was dark excerpt for a noticeable light flickering through the windows on the fourth floor.

"Maison Duchamp," Emma said and her eyes widened. She braced her hand against one of the posts flanking the stairs leading off the porch. "That's you, *Duchamp*. Did you used to own that?"

"With my husband, yes."

It was the cold case Emma had glanced at only that morning. The hotel with the ghost who couldn't be exorcised, couldn't be found at all. So many agents had investigated the location, but found no evidence of a haunting. However, anyone who'd bought the property insisted that it was haunted. Supposedly, the ghost was very unfriendly, driving away business so they couldn't make enough money to stay open.

"Is your husband the ghost that haunts Maison Duchamp?" Emma asked.

"He is." Lorraine nodded.

"No one's ever established that he's really there. No one can locate him to even talk to him."

"Harold always enjoyed playing hide and seek."

"Why is he there and you're here?"

"I don't know. But I can feel him. I know he's there and I know he's very unhappy. I can't leave here or I'd go to him. It's frustrating." She looked beseechingly at Emma. "Can you help me?"

"Of course we can," Ryan said.

Emma turned to him with a look of surprise. "What did you say?"

"I said of course we can help her."

"How can you see or hear her? You're not clairvoyant." She looked at Lorraine.

The ghost shrugged. "I can show myself to whomever I please, whether or not they have the sight. People like you are the ones who can see me no matter what, that's all. Those who have come here before haven't been as nice as you, so I've avoided them."

Emma blinked. "You think I can help you because I'm *nice.*"

"I was talking about him, actually."

Emma glanced at Ryan, then back at the ghost. "I thought you said he was trouble."

Lorraine smiled. "Doesn't mean I don't like him."

"See, Em?" Ryan grinned. "My charm transcends death. Why can't you admit it yourself?"

"It's incredible, actually," Lorraine said. "I can feel such electricity between you. It's so strong, it's like a thread binding you together."

Emma felt it, but she wasn't acknowledging it.

Ryan crossed his arms over his chest. "It's the lust potion. It must be noticeable on a celestial level."

Lorraine raised her eyebrows. "No wonder the other man was so jealous. Reminds me of my Harold."

"Leo reminds you of Harold?" Emma shifted her purse higher up on her shoulder.

"No, this one does." She nodded at Ryan.

"Charming, funny and lovable?" he offered.

"Self-loathing, secretive and a pain in the butt," she said, but then smiled. "And worth every moment of the trouble."

"I am a pain in the butt," Ryan agreed. "But I'm not self-loathing."

"If you say so."

"I love myself. Actually, I've been doing that a bit too often lately. I seriously need to date more."

Emma repressed a smile. "Listen, Lorraine, I do want to help, but I'm not sure if I can. People from our agency have been trying to talk to your husband for years, but couldn't find him. That means he's strong enough to stay hidden."

She shook her head. "They haven't ever visited him on our anniversary."

"Which means?"

"He'll talk. If you mention me, he'll talk." Her smile faded. "Just be careful. His temper...it can get a little much. I was able to calm him, but I haven't seen him for so long that he might be dangerous." Lorraine's eyes again shone with tears. "Tell Harold that I'm still waiting. That I'll keep waiting, forever, if that's what it takes. And...that I forgive him for what he did and I still love him, even after all this time."

Without another word, she faded away.

Ryan looked at her. "So do you really want to do this?"

"Ghost hunting without the hunting?"

He smiled and it was enough to weaken her knees. "Just like old times."

"Are you saying you want to come with me?"

"Absolutely. If there's a dangerous ghost then you'll need a bodyguard. And you know I'm more than willing to guard your body."

He moved closer to her and she backed up until she was pressed against a pillar. "Ryan…"

"Yes, Emma?" He was so close that the heat from his body sank deeply into hers.

She couldn't concentrate. The effects of the Desidero potion swirled between them. It took everything in her not to reach for him, pull him against her, and crush her mouth against his.

It was a losing battle, because she'd already touched him, her hand pressed against his chest. His heartbeat felt fast beneath her touch.

"Being close to each other—" she said in a husky voice.

"Won't be a problem. I swear to stay at least ten feet away from you at all times so you aren't…distracted."

"I'm distracted right now."

"Yeah?" He leaned over a little so their gazes were on the same level.

"Why did you come here, Ryan?"

"To this restaurant or to Mystic Ridge?"

"Both."

His warm breath touched her cheek as he leaned closer to whisper in her ear. "Because the memory of your mouth on me drives me so crazy that I can't stop thinking about you."

She knew she should pull away from him, but she couldn't. She felt the hard ridge of his erection against her hip as he pressed her back against the pillar.

She wanted him. Damn it, she wanted him more than anything. It was almost enough to make her push all of her convictions aside.

Almost.

If they hadn't been interrupted by the knock at Xavier's library door the other night, then there was no doubt in her mind she would have done more than just had oral sex with Ryan right then and there.

Her desire for Ryan had needed release when they'd been partners—so she'd written it all down in her book. She'd thought that had been it, that she'd gotten it out forever so it wouldn't stay with her. She'd decided one book was all it would take. But lately she'd been itching to write more. Her fantasies seemed to multiply the more she tried to hold them back.

And they were all about Ryan. Even before she'd seen him again. Even before the potion had taken its hold on her.

But the writing didn't pay the bills. That was her real job, PARA. And she knew screwing things up with the potion bottle would be a negative mark on her career.

She could make up for it, though. Tonight.

Cracking a cold case would definitely earn her extra points when it came time for her review. She might even be promoted within the company and her future as an agent would be solidified.

Emma did want to help Lorraine if she could. She liked using her ability to help spirits trapped on earth, especially those dealing with broken hearts. She was a sucker for a love story.

"I'll go. But this changes nothing between us," she managed to say calmly. It took every ounce of strength inside her to push away from him. Her face felt hot and her body ached. Just a taste had only increased her appetite for Ryan.

He nodded. "I get it. You still hate me. You don't trust me. Et cetera."

"As long as we're clear on that."

"Totally clear."

There was never any question about helping the ghost out. Emma *was* a romantic. She'd seen that pained look in Lorraine's eyes. The woman missed her husband desperately. Even though the guy was self-loathing, secretive and a pain in the butt.

He was like Ryan. Her former partner might deny the self-loathing, but she'd seen it in his expression at the party. There was a part of him that hated what he'd done. She knew that he missed his life as a PARA agent. If he regretted his past actions, maybe that would make a difference. Maybe he'd finally own up to it. And maybe then she could finally forgive him.

Emma reminded herself that she shouldn't care one way or the other, but she did. She couldn't deny it. She cared about Ryan and she didn't want him to be unhappy.

Everyone made their own choices in life. Some were big ones, and others were small. The problem was, at the time you made a choice, you were never sure which category it fell into. A small choice might lead to large consequences that would haunt you for the rest of your life.

Literal hauntings were a lot easier to deal with. Even when they involved potentially dangerous ghosts.

Emma shifted her purse to her other shoulder and eyed the hotel which stood about two blocks away from the restaurant. She didn't have to look to see that Ryan had moved closer to her side again. Her heart pounded faster when he pressed his hand against her back.

"What are you doing?" she asked, a breathy quality to her voice.

"I'm sorry."

"What for?"

Ryan's expression had become strained. "I said I'd keep ten feet between us, but it's more difficult than I thought. I'm finding it nearly impossible not to touch you."

"A promise is a promise."

"Look at me, Em."

She didn't want to, but she moved as if her body had a mind of its own.

"What?" she asked.

"Are you going to see Leo again after tonight?" He appeared very serious all of a sudden.

She couldn't help it, she had to laugh at that. "Why are you asking?"

"I don't like him. You can do better."

"He's fairly perfect."

"That's probably what I don't like about him. If you're going to date someone, then he should be a bit rough around the edges. He shouldn't be perfect. Perfect is boring."

"I'll definitely take your suggestion under advisement." He was still touching her, and his touch burned into her skin through the thin material of her teal blouse. Desire twisted inside her and it was impossible to ignore. He had her encircled in his arms, his hands low on her back. She felt the urge to lean against him and feel his body press against hers again. He watched every move she made as if memorizing her actions for later reference. His gaze moved to her lips.

"Do you have any idea how much I want to kiss you right now?" he asked. "And how crazy it made me to see *him* kiss you?"

"Ryan…"

"This potion will wear off soon, I promise. Until then…"

She struggled to breathe. She could feel his warm breath against her face, his lips only an inch from hers. "Until then what?"

His hands slid lower, his fingers digging into the soft curve of her buttocks through her skirt. She felt herself grow damp between her legs and her body ached for him to touch her much more intimately.

His mouth brushed against hers. Not a kiss, exactly. Just a touch. "Until then you're going to have to be strong for both of us. I talk a good game, but I know you'd regret it. I don't want you to hate me any more than you already do."

When he let go of her, she realized that she'd been gripping his sides. Her face felt flushed and there was an emptiness inside her that felt cold. She'd wanted him so much, she'd nearly forgotten herself. Again.

This didn't feel like just lust, this pull Ryan had on her. It felt much bigger and deeper and much more apt to tear her life completely apart if she gave into this growing need she had for the man who'd broken her heart six months ago.

Now *that* was a scary thought.

"Let's go," Ryan said, putting a little distance between them. "We need to have a chat with a ghost."

7

In its time, Maison Duchamp had been a very popular hotel in Mystic Ridge. Emma racked her mind trying to remember everything she'd read about the place. It had been closed for as long as she'd lived here—and that was going on five years now. That had been the last time it had been fully investigated. Without owners to request—and pay for—PARA's services, the property remained untouched, its file put into the cold case pile.

Still, Patrick would definitely appreciate a quick result. And if Emma could deliver that when so many others had failed, then she knew it would mean good things for her future.

She sensed it without much concentration. Lorraine might be nice and friendly, but her husband wasn't the type who looked forward to entertaining guests. That light flickering on the fourth floor was not the most welcome sight Emma had ever seen.

"I don't have any exorcism paraphernalia," she whispered.

Ryan glanced at her. "I didn't know that was a possibility."

"I'd prefer not to have to go to those extremes, but if he's too much to handle…"

"If he's too much to handle, we'll just leave. All we're doing is checking this out and letting Lorraine know what we find. She's looking for peace of mind before she'll move on. Her peace of mind seems to be entirely centered around this husband of hers."

He looked at the front door after following her up the five steps leading up to it. True to his word earlier, he was attempting to keep some space between them. He knew that if he got too close, she'd have a hard time keeping her mind on business. And with a case like this, she didn't need any distractions.

She turned the knob but failed. "It's locked."

"Got a couple bobby pins?"

She raised an eyebrow. "You're kidding."

"Not at the moment."

Emma pulled the pins out of her hair that were keeping her long bangs back from her face. She'd spent an hour getting ready for her date tonight, but her hair hadn't been co-operating. She handed the pins to Ryan and watched him skeptically as he stretched them out, then inserted them into the lock and began wiggling them around.

"Picking locks," she observed dryly. "What a huge surprise."

"I'm a man of many hidden skills."

"I have no doubt about that."

He looked at her as if realizing he'd admitted to something illegal. "This might not work. I haven't done it in a long time."

"I don't even want to know where you picked it up."

"I locked myself out of my house once upon a time."

"Sure."

He grinned. "I know you think I'm a master criminal,

but I haven't hotwired a car since I was a teenager. This is as bad as it gets."

She was about to say something when she heard a click. Ryan turned the knob and the door swung inward.

He waved a hand at the dark interior of the hotel. "After you, madam."

She ventured past him slowly, ignoring the momentary swell of lust she felt when she got too close to him. After all, she'd almost lost what few inhibitions she still had left just outside the restaurant only minutes ago. She couldn't deal with that again now.

She'd swept her gaze around the hotel lobby. It was dark, but she could see outlines of furniture under plastic wrap. There was a check-in desk with mail slots behind it. A staircase rose up at the far end of the lobby leading to the second floor. It smelled musty, but not as much as she might have thought.

No security system. She'd half expected a siren to blare, but there was only silence.

No, not complete silence. She could hear something very faintly.

"Do you hear that?" she whispered.

"Do I—?" Ryan cocked his head. "Yeah, music. Upstairs. It sounds like something from the thirties or forties."

"Harold's listening to some old tunes." She looked at the staircase in front of them. "Let's go."

Ryan frowned. "You're sure you want to confront him? Why not just give a report to PARA tomorrow? You said you didn't have any exorcism stuff on you."

Even as a child Emma would seek spirits out, as if drawn to haunted locations like a magnet. Sometimes they were tricky to talk to, but it was always because they had some struggle, some issue they still were dealing with. It was a vicious cycle for them until somebody—like Emma—was able to knock them out of their repeating pattern.

It had worked before. It would work again. She was sure of it.

Ryan was concerned for her safety, which was why he had caught her arm just as she'd placed her stiletto-clad foot on the first step. She appreciated that concern more than he knew, but it didn't change anything. The Desidero potion's effects continued to swirl around her, making it very hard to keep her head clear enough to do her job.

"It's their anniversary tonight," she explained. "Lorraine said he'll be in hiding any other time. This is it if we want to help them."

Ryan studied her face, his mouth curving. "There's that stubborn streak I remember."

"I'm not stubborn."

"Hey, it was a compliment, not an insult. Maybe you should have brought Leo along. How many times have you been out with that guy, anyway? Is he your boyfriend?"

She glanced down at where Ryan had his hand curled over her forearm. The contact was so pleasant it made her struggle against the need to get closer to him. "You seem very interested in him. I'll have to ask if he's interested in seeing *you* again. Maybe you can be a couple."

"So funny I forgot to laugh. You're avoiding the question. Are you into that guy or what?"

"It was our first date," Emma admitted, not sure why she was even answering him.

"Has there been anyone else since I left?"

"Why do you care?" She twisted a finger through her hair.

His smile widened. "Isn't it obvious? I'm insanely jealous."

She placed her hand on top of his and removed it from her arm so she could focus on the task facing her. "It wasn't as if we were involved when you were here, Ryan. You were dating Charlotte. You were my business partner, that's all."

"Seems like a million years ago." He scanned the empty lobby, before his gaze moved up the stairway they had yet to climb. "How is Charlotte, anyway?"

Strange that he hadn't asked about her until now. "Never better."

"She moved on, I assume."

"From you?"

"Yeah. She didn't seem the type to pine away."

Emma nodded. "She's seeing someone else."

"Do I know him?"

"Actually, yes. It's Stephen."

His eyes widened. "Stephen *Robbins?*"

"The one and only."

He laughed under his breath. "That son of a bitch moved in on Charlotte the moment I was out of the picture, didn't he?"

Stephen and Ryan had been friends while Ryan worked for the agency. Stephen had been shocked as hell to find out that Ryan was a thief, possibly even more than Emma herself had been. She and Stephen hadn't been close so they couldn't commiserate, but he and Charlotte had started seeing each other soon afterward. And they seemed to be very serious about each other now.

"I guess you two haven't stayed in touch," she said.

"No, strangely enough, nobody wanted anything to do with me after I left. I'm like a leper. Charlotte didn't even say goodbye. At least you said a few parting words to me."

"I believe I told you to go to hell."

He smiled. "At least it was an acknowledgment that I was leaving."

Emma searched his face. "Do you feel bad about what happened?"

His expression shadowed and his smile faded. "You have no idea how bad I feel about it."

There was pain in his eyes, but it quickly disappeared. It was something, though. Something she could hold on to. She felt like a bit of a masochist for wanting him to feel bad, but it was better than if he'd been completely blasé about it. Ryan definitely wasn't blasé.

"You know," she said, thinking things through. "If you were to recover the stolen merchandise and return it, it's possible things might be different."

He snorted, but it was a humorless sound. "You think?"

"I do."

"If I knew where everything was, then that might be possible. But I don't."

"You could go back to the people you sold the items to and—"

He cut her off. "You just don't get it, do you, Em?"

"Get what?"

He stared at her for a long, drawn-out moment. She could sense the tension building between them wasn't merely sexual anymore. "I didn't steal anything."

She frowned. "But—"

"No, Em, it wasn't me. I was set up to take the fall." He looked frustrated.

Her jaw tightened and disappointment flooded through her. "I see."

His brows drew together. "A part of you has to see that I'm innocent. I'd never do something like that."

"Let's just forget I said anything."

She tried to ignore the lump that quickly formed in her throat. Even *now* he was denying it. But she remembered it so clearly, it was as if it had been only yesterday, watching him around the corner of the building as he left the office with a duffle bag in hand. He'd looked suspicious and checked his surroundings, then unloaded the bag into the trunk of a car. He got on his cell phone and spoke to somebody on the other end.

"I have the items," he said. "Nobody even saw me. Meet me at the rendezvous point in ten minutes for the handoff."

That didn't sound like an innocent phone call to Emma.

She'd wondered why Ryan hadn't sensed any suspicion from her the next day. He was an empath, after all, although it took a lot of concentration for him to get a good read on anyone. Looked like he hadn't wanted to expend any extra energy on Emma.

The vault might have been easy to break into, but it had been equipped with a security camera. It had captured a glimpse of the perpetrator. It had been enough to turn attention toward Ryan.

Patrick knew about Ryan's history as a car thief—a story told one night over drinks at the pub down the street. That hadn't helped his case, especially not when a witness confirmed that it had definitely been Ryan on the security tape.

In confidence, Emma had told Patrick what she'd seen. In return, he'd kept her name out of matters. Patrick, as agency manager, had had no choice but to fire Ryan. He'd done it privately, but word spread like wildfire.

Ryan had no idea that it was Emma who'd been the nail in his coffin. But her disappointment with him had been so vast, her trust in a partner that she'd had extremely warm feelings for so shattered, that she couldn't help herself. It had felt like her father's betrayal all over again. Perhaps he'd only taken the job at PARA so he could steal from the vault on a regular basis.

Then, instead of just admitting it and doing what he could to fix the situation, Ryan continued to claim his innocence.

And despite this, she still wanted him. Forget the lust potion that made it impossible for her to deny her attraction to him, she still desired him even without it—desired a man who'd lied to her and betrayed her. Even now she wanted to forget about the past and give him a chance to make it up to her.

But she'd be setting herself up for more disappointment. She knew it. It had been proven one too many times before.

Her feelings were definitely complicated, especially now. She hated what he'd done, but she wanted him anyway.

And she knew that was not the least bit healthy.

"Come on," she said, starting up the stairs. "Let's get this over with."

He stood at the base of the stairway with his hands on his hips. "So, what? You're just going to confront Harold?"

"Yeah, that's pretty much it." After this was over, she wanted to go home. Alone. Then she'd try her very best to put Ryan out of her head and wait for the lust potion's affects to fade away. She'd researched the potion earlier that day at the office. The effects would wane if given enough time. A week, maybe. Giving in to their desires would allegedly help speed the process along, but…that wasn't a good idea. It would cause too many complications.

Writing about him in her erotic novel had been cathartic, but ultimately unhelpful. She knew that now. It just kept him vividly in her mind as an object of desire. A scene she'd written when her characters had made love in a bedroom filled with candles and red roses flickered in her mind. It was the scene when her heroine realized that the hero wasn't only interested in sex. He'd fallen in love with her.

It was only a fantasy. And that was how it would stay, no matter how much her body ached to feel Ryan's against hers. This lust potion was only a temporary problem. Ryan's presence in her life again was only a temporary problem. She just had to be strong for a little while longer.

So instead, she thought about the job in front of her. She'd dealt with a lot of ghosts in her life. And nine times out of ten, they were reasonable sorts, if a bit confused about what had happened to them.

Emma and Ryan finally reached the fourth floor which had a banister along one side of the hallway, showing a open view down to the lobby. All the lights on this floor were flickering, even the ones set into the ceiling.

"I'd be surprised if they'd even paid the electricity bill recently," Ryan said. "After all, nobody's running this place anymore."

"This is all because of Harold," Emma agreed. "It shows that he's aggravated and highly emotional. It's enough to affect the power levels around him and in this particular case, it's electricity."

"Great."

Normally she'd hang back a little and get her bearings, trying to sense the ghost and predict what he might do.

But she was on edge and she wanted this over with. With Ryan a bit too close for comfort, she began to open doors into the rooms that looked as if they'd been frozen in time. Each one was identical with a double bed, a wooden desk, a chair, and a window with green curtains.

"Where is he?" Ryan asked. "Do you sense him at all?"

She did. He was here. He was watching them.

"Harold Duchamp," she called out. "My name is Emma Black and this is Ryan Shephard. Please show yourself to us."

There was silence for a moment, and then a loud, deep voice boomed, "You're not welcome here."

"We're here to help you. You don't have to hide from us, we mean you no harm."

"Leave me to suffer in peace!"

A door at the far end of the hallway flew open and something launched out of it. A glass vase. Ryan grabbed Emma and pulled her out of the way before it smashed against the wall behind her.

She inhaled sharply. "Well, so much for Casper the Friendly Ghost."

"Watch out!" Ryan yanked Emma against him as a wooden chair rocketed past them.

"He's not all that open to meeting new people," Emma said

"You think?"

"This ghost has serious anger issues."

Ryan looked angry, too. "Not such a romantic tale of love and loss anymore, is it? Lorraine should be glad to see the end of him."

Maybe this was a mistake. She wanted to solve the case so she'd be looked at in a better light at PARA, but the ghost of Harold Duchamp was making it clear he meant to physically harm them. With the lust she felt for Ryan clouding her thoughts, she definitely wasn't on her game tonight.

Unfortunately, an exorcism was impossible. She had a bag in the trunk of her car at her house that held everything she needed for that—candles, salt, a exorcist handbook that contained all of the incantations she could recite. She'd never managed to memorize them since exorcisms were fairly rare. She hadn't done one in over a year. Most ghosts were not evil, after all. They were usually more than open to moving on once the situation had been properly explained to them. Those like Lorraine were still trapped in this world because they were tied to someone or something. In this case, it seemed to be her husband.

Ryan and Emma went down the stairs as quickly as they could. They looked up and could see the doors slamming on the fourth floor. Emma could now feel Harold's growing rage like it was a palpable thing.

The front door was still open but as they made their way across the lobby, it slammed shut in front of them.

Ryan grabbed hold of the handle and shot a look at her over his shoulder. "I can't open it."

Now the lights in the lobby, including those of a large chandelier high above them began to flicker violently. The sofa and two armchairs, all under a layer of protective plastic, began to shake, as if there was an earthquake rolling under their feet. The dark fireplace suddenly began to blaze right before their eyes.

Emma looked at Ryan and she could see the worry etched into his handsome features.

They'd angered a ghost. And the ghost was ready to take his revenge.

8

RYAN TRIED TO REMEMBER whose idea it had been to come here and confront this pissed-off spirit. He had a funny feeling it might have been his.

Bad idea.

He reached for Emma, closing his hand around her wrist. She looked at him and he could see a mix of emotions in her eyes. The lust potion made it difficult to think about anything other than having her, especially when he was actually touching her skin to skin, but he willed himself to remain in control of his body and mind.

"It's okay," she assured him, without much conviction.

"This isn't okay. Just stay behind me."

She looked at him incredulously. "You're going to protect me from the big bad ghost?"

"That was my plan. Your mocking of my plan doesn't help matters much."

"I'm the clairvoyant here." Her black high heels dug into the red carpet.

"You are."

"Did you hear him upstairs?"

"He spoke?"

"Yeah, he did. He said he wanted to be alone so he could suffer in peace. So he's here and he knows who we are. I just need to get him to talk to us."

"Before or after he kills us?"

"Hopefully before. We're lucky he didn't push us off that landing up there." She looked determined, and the fear he'd seen on her face a minute ago seemed to have disappeared. Her jaw set. "It's okay, Ryan. I think this guy may be more bark than bite."

"We'll have to disagree on that."

"You're going to have to let go of me."

He shook his head, but released her wrist and took her by the upper arms, pulling her closer to him. "Not a chance."

She inhaled sharply. "Touching me is distracting."

"Tell me about it." His gaze swept over her and he noticed the impression the hard peaks of her nipples made against the thin silk of her blouse. Despite their current situation, this evidence of her arousal made his mouth water and his cock grow hard. "Damn it."

"What?" She sounded breathless.

"You're so damn beautiful, Em. You know that?"

"Ryan—" She shook her head. "This isn't a good time."

"I can't help it." He swore under his breath. "I want you so much it hurts."

She glared at him, but her gaze wasn't filled with the usual malice. Instead, he saw confusion mixed with heated desire. She couldn't figure him out. She still believed that he was a thief. He knew there wasn't a shadow of doubt in her mind about that. What did he have to do to prove his innocence?

Openly staring at her breasts probably wasn't a good start.

Still, he didn't want to let go of her. He'd pledged to stay by her side, to protect her from danger. That wasn't exactly the behavior of a thief and liar.

The fact that she was confused right now was the first glimmer of hope he'd felt in a very long time. And the heated look she'd given him a moment ago was bringing his blood to a steady boil. He knew it was dangerous to touch her, but he'd be damned if he was going to let her wander off in a haunted house that was home to a belligerent ghost.

Still, he was disappointed that she wasn't willing to take him at his word. He wondered exactly what he'd done to convince her that he couldn't be trusted.

He wanted to pull her to him, to kiss her until she believed him, to slide his mouth and tongue over every inch of her sexy body until she screamed his name and begged him to make love to her.

Emma finally broke eye contact, a flush now on her cheeks. If he didn't know better, he'd think that she'd read his mind and seen everything he wanted to do to her. Many of the things were already detailed in that sexy novel he'd read.

He'd be very happy to bring every last one of her fantasies to life if she gave him half a chance.

"Harold Duchamp," Emma said, after pushing away from him. She stared around at the lobby filled with shaking furniture and flickering lights. Her voice didn't tremble, it sounded out strong and commanding. He was impressed and he watched her full lips form the words. Everything she did, every move she made, now seemed painfully erotic to him. They'd been too close for too long and the potion's effects were impossible to ignore. "I am not afraid of you," she continued. "I demand that you show yourself immediately—to both of us."

The shaking and tremors increased and the noise was so loud that Ryan had the urge to cover his ears with his hands but he didn't budge. The only sign that Emma was anything but totally calm was the fact that she was now squeezing his hand very tightly. He admired her hidden strength and tried to refrain from flinching in pain.

Finally the form of a man slowly began to solidify in front of them. He looked to be in his thirties, with brown hair trimmed short, a handsome face, a well-groomed beard and moustache, and a suit that also appeared—much like Lorraine's dress and appearance—to be something from the 1940s.

Harold glared at them. "I warned you."

Even though he'd seen Lorraine, Ryan was surprised he was able to see this ghost as well. When he and Emma had been partners, he hadn't once seen a ghost. Emma had taken care of things all by herself, while Ryan typically assured the scared homeowners that everything would be okay, doing his best to sense their emotions. Fear was one of the easiest emotions to sense empathically, even if the person was trying to hide it.

Like now. He could tell that Emma was afraid. He felt it coming off her in waves. It helped to give him additional courage. He'd protect her, no matter what.

"You told us to leave," Emma said evenly to Harold. "But then you locked the front door, trapping us in here with you."

"Perhaps I wanted to teach you a lesson."

"By killing us?"

His gaze narrowed and he drew closer, eyeing them both with distaste as if they were maggots he'd found on the underside of a loaf of bread. "Why have you disturbed me tonight? What right do you have to be here?"

Emma drew in a shaky breath. "Happy anniversary."

Harold grew transparent for a moment before his form became opaque again. Ryan guessed it was his way of showing intense surprise.

"Excuse me?" he snapped.

"I know it's your anniversary tonight."

Harold looked ill. "And how would you know something like that?"

"Because I spoke with your wife, Lorraine."

The ghost's mouth fell open and pain flashed in his gaze. "It's not possible. She's gone."

"No, she's not. She's close. Actually, she's just a few hundred yards away from this building. Her spirit is trapped in a restaurant that used to be an old house."

Harold glanced in the direction Emma pointed, toward the locked door. There were windows on either side, but they were covered with thick curtains. "Our house. But no…it's not possible."

"Why?"

"I would have known. I would have sensed her—seen her. All of these years, there's no way she could have been that close and I wouldn't have known it."

"She's close. Trust us."

"Why should I trust you? I don't know you." His eyes narrowed.

Emma's grip hadn't loosened a bit from Ryan's hand. "She wanted me to tell you something…"

"What?" Harold searched her face.

"That she forgives you."

His eyes narrowed and a hateful look filled his expression. "You're a liar."

He moved toward Emma quickly and Ryan yanked her back, placing himself directly in front of her. He hadn't consciously thought about it first, it had been an automatic reflex.

"Don't even think about it," Ryan growled.

Harold stopped in his tracks, glaring at Ryan for a moment before a cold smile crossed his face. "You think you can stop me if I mean to do anything? This is my territory and no one is welcome here."

"Can I stop a ghost who's being a complete and utter asshole?" Ryan's jaw tightened. "I'll sure as hell try. If you so much as make a move toward Emma I will make your afterlife even more hellish than it already is."

Harold glowered at him. "I don't fear you."

Ryan returned the sour look with one of his own. "What's your problem, anyway? You have a woman who has been pining away for your sorry ass for the last seventy years, yet you stay here, flickering lights all by yourself, because you want to suffer?"

"What damned business is it of yours what I choose to do?"

"Isolating yourself is not something anyone would choose. Trust me on that." It hit a bit close to home, actually.

"You're trying to tell me that you know how I feel?" Harold's words dripped sarcasm. "That is highly un-likely."

"Yeah, all alone. All by your sorry self. Not much fun, is it?" Ryan's words twisted with the irony he felt. He'd been alone for far too long, but it wasn't entirely by choice. He thought it through, his brow furrowing. "Wait a minute, I think I'm getting it."

"I doubt that."

Ryan's gaze flicked to the ghost. "You're here, all by yourself. In this hotel." He looked around the lobby with the high ceiling, up to the floors with open banisters on the landings looking down to this area. The furniture had stopped shaking but the lights still flickered ominously. "Your wife still loves you. Her soul is tied to yours. That doesn't happen very often. If you weren't that important to her, she would have been able to move on without you. You did something you feel guilty for—so guilty that you can't get over it."

Emma looked at him, her eyes wide. "You're right."

"Of course I am." He gave her a grin before forcing himself to look at the angry ghost again.

Harold just glared at him, then he turned his back and walked away, not climbing the stairs as much as *floating* up them.

"Where do you think you're going?" Ryan let go of Emma's hand and chased after the ghost. Emma was right behind him.

"To my room, where I belong," Harold said without turning around.

They followed him up the stairs again to the fourth floor, watching as Harold disappeared through a wall into a room with a closed door. To their right was the wooden banister that looked down to the lobby. Higher up, the large chandelier flickered ominously from where it hung from the very center of the ceiling. Ryan tried the handle of the door and wasn't surprised to find it locked. He looked over his shoulder at Emma.

"So now what?" he asked.

"I honestly don't know. I'm open to suggestion. Exorcism? Maybe come back a little later?"

"No." Ryan pressed his hand against the closed door. "This guy isn't bad to the bone. He's just misunderstood, even by himself."

"Which means what?"

"He's still in love with his wife. That's why their

anniversary is such a big deal. But something's keeping them apart. Something he feels he did wrong. He's punishing himself for it."

Emma looked at him quizzically. "How do you know he's still in love with her? I didn't think you could sense any emotion from spirits."

"I can't. But I saw it in his eyes when you mentioned her name. He looked like it was tearing him up inside. And there's only one thing that can do something like that."

"And that's guilt?"

"Yes."

Emma leaned against the railing across from him and glanced down to the lobby before returning her attention to Ryan, her face bathed in shadows. "What's he guilty of?"

Ryan wracked his mind. "I don't know. But something has been eating away at him for all of these years and keeping him from the woman he loves."

"Wait a sec." Emma frowned.

"What is it?"

She glanced around the hallway, the long mirror along the wall, the peeling wallpaper, the red carpet, the banister she held on to. Her gaze finally fell on the door of Harold's room.

"Something's happening. I can feel the energy growing in there. His anger is manifesting…"

Ryan frowned. "Manifesting into what?"

Her face was pale. "Something bad."

Suddenly the door Ryan stood in front of burst open and what felt like a blast of energy exited like a metaphysical punch.

The railing Emma leaned against splintered and fell away like it hadn't been more solid than cardboard. It was the only thing between the fourth-floor landing and the drop to the open lobby far below.

Emma shrieked as she lost her footing and began to fall.

Ryan didn't think, he simply reacted, closing the distance between them in a split second. He grabbed for Emma's hand just as part of the broken wooden banister crashed to the ground floor.

Emma dangled off the landing, staring up at him with fear. Harold's anger had hit them like a wave of powerful negative energy. He'd been trying to kill Emma.

"Don't let go of me!" she cried.

"I won't."

"You shouldn't have come here," Harold was suddenly beside Ryan, looking down at Emma as she scrambled to keep a hold on Ryan's hand. There was a mix of guilt and fury on the ghost's face. "I should be alone, always alone. I don't need the reminder of what I've destroyed with my mistakes."

"Shut the hell up," Ryan snarled. He needed to focus all his concentration or Emma was going to slip through his grasp and fall sixty feet to the lobby floor. "Give me your other hand. Now, Emma. Do it!"

Their gazes locked and there was a sheen of perspiration on her forehead. One of her high-heeled shoes fell off her right foot and fell to the ground. She reached up with her other hand and he grasped it tightly.

He forgot about absolutely everything else—his troubles with PARA, his weak psychic ability, his search for the truth, the lust potion that made everything that much more difficult and tempting being around Emma. None of that mattered. If he let Emma fall, he may as well join Harold here and become a selfish, self-hating ghost who craved solitude.

He wouldn't let her slip. He held on so tightly to her, he was sure he was bruising her wrists, but it was a small price to pay. Inch by inch he pulled her back up to the landing. He crushed her against his chest in a tight embrace.

"That was too close," he whispered into her hair, which he brushed back from her face so he could look into her green eyes. She was hugging him back just as fiercely. "Are you okay?"

She just nodded. "That was close."

"Too damn close."

He pulled her to him and kissed her, hot and deep and open-mouthed. She gasped against his lips before kissing him back. There was no way she wouldn't be able to feel his erection pressing into her, telling her clearly just how damn much he wanted her. His tongue slid against hers and he heard someone groan deep in their throat. He thought it was probably him.

After a moment, he released her, though she kept hold of his arm. Harold waited close by, his face twisted with grief and misery.

"When I get angry, bad things happen," he said bleakly. "I can't control it. I'm so sorry."

Ryan's hands curled into fists. "What did you do, Harold?"

"Excuse me?"

"Seventy years ago, or however long ago you died. What did you do that Lorraine would have to forgive you for? What is it that you still hate yourself for doing that keeps you stuck here all alone, all these years later, unable to find the peace you need to move on?"

Harold was silent for a long moment, his face etched in pain and regret and guilt. "I lost so much money gambling—Lorraine begged me to stop, but I couldn't.

I knew if I hit it, we'd be on easy street for the rest of our lives."

Emma and Ryan exchanged a glance.

"But you didn't," Ryan said.

His expression shadowed. "No. The bills were mounting up higher and higher every day. It was too much for me—for her. She lost our baby because of the stress." His expression twisted with pain.

"I'm sorry," Emma said, and there was a catch of emotion in her voice. Ryan fisted his hands at his sides to keep from drawing her close to him again.

Harold nodded, pain etched into his face. "So I did what any man who'd been driven half mad by the thought that I couldn't support my family would do."

"You killed yourself," Ryan guessed.

That earned him a sharp glare. "No. I wanted to give my wife everything she deserved, everything I could never afford for her. So…I stupidly decided to rob a bank right here in Mystic Ridge. I went in with a gun— no bullets. I never wanted to hurt anyone, I just needed cash."

Emma stayed silent and let Harold tell his story, staying clear of the broken banister. Ryan leaned against the wall next to the mirror behind him. He couldn't get an empathic read on a dead person, but by the look on Harold's face, he was telling the truth as he remembered it.

"Then what happened?" Ryan prompted when Harold went silent.

"Got tens of thousands stuffed in a bag and I headed home to take Lorraine on a long vacation." The small grin that played at his mouth at the pleasant part of his memory vanished completely. "Lorraine asked me where

I got the money and I lied to her. I told her I'd inherited it and it had just been wired to me. And…she believed me."

"She loved you," Emma said.

This statement only made Harold look more distraught. "The cops came for me when she was packing a couple suitcases for us. Lorraine, she—she tried to protect me, stood in front of me and told the cops what I'd told her. That I couldn't have robbed a bank, that it was inheritance money. She got in the way when they pulled the trigger, and then—" His voice broke and he drew in a ragged breath. A silvery tear slipped down his cheek.

Emma inhaled shakily. Ryan glanced at her to see that her eyes were glassy. It was painful, but Ryan knew she had to get the ghost to tell his story, to deal with what was keeping him earthbound for so many years. It was the only way, other than exorcism, to deal with a haunting like this.

"It happened on our anniversary," Harold said. "She died in my arms. I was so furious that I stormed at the cop with my gun held up and he shot me without hesitating. Both of us dead because of my stupid mistake. Now I'm here, in the hotel that I couldn't keep going—our nest egg. Everything I chose led to pain and death. And every year on our anniversary I feel that pain like it was only yesterday."

Emma's face had paled. Ryan moved to put his arm around her. It was worth the risk of contact. He still wasn't certain that Harold could control himself. Ghosts held a whole lot more power than even they were aware of, especially when they were distraught.

"Harold," Emma said after a minute of silence passed between them. "Look at me. Please."

He raised his gaze to hers and there wasn't anger in his eyes anymore, only sadness.

"Lorraine specifically told me that she forgives you. No matter what happened, she forgives you. And she loves you. She's waited all this time for you to forgive yourself. For you to return to her. But you're delaying her peace and happiness—*your* peace and happiness—because you won't forgive yourself."

He frowned deeply. "I don't understand."

"You need to forgive yourself for what you did," Emma said, raw emotion in her voice. "Forgive yourself and go to her. Don't you see that this day—your anniversary, the day that you died—has power in it? I could feel it the moment I set foot in here. She can't leave where she is because it's not her decision. It's yours."

Harold looked defeated. "I can't leave this hotel."

"Have you ever tried?"

His jaw set, he looked down at the floor and shook his head.

"She loves you—that's not something that should just be ignored! Do you still love her?"

"Of course I do." His voice broke.

"Then go to her," Emma said firmly. "And stop wasting more precious time."

Harold glanced at Ryan who still stood warily watching the ghost, barely believing what he'd seen with his own eyes.

Finally, Harold nodded. "I could see our house from the fourth floor. That's why I stayed up there. I had no idea she was waiting for me all this time. I couldn't see her."

"You didn't want to see her. You were afraid. But it's time for you to gather your courage and go to her."

Ryan nodded. "She's waiting for you."

Harold raked a ghostly hand through his hair. "Thank you."

Then he faded from sight.

Emma let out a shaky sigh and looked at Ryan. She was smiling. "Come on." She grabbed his hand and pulled him into the room in front of them. They stood by the window and looked across the way toward the restaurant.

"Can you see her?" Emma asked, leaning against Ryan's side.

He squinted at the distance. Yes, he could. Lorraine stood on the veranda of the restaurant—the veranda of the house she'd shared with Harold. A pale silver glow approached her and it solidified into Harold's form. He ran up the stairs and embraced his wife.

Then, only a few moments later, they both disappeared in a soft flash of light.

"So what does that mean?" Ryan asked. "They found their peace? They've moved on?"

Emma didn't answer. It was dark in the room, the lights had stopped flickering. She stared at his face.

"What's wrong?" he asked.

"It makes you think, doesn't it? About wasting time worrying so damn much about what's right and what's wrong? Sometimes we just need a bit of a reminder, don't we?"

"What do you mean?"

She slid her hands over his shoulders and up into his hair. Thanks to their proximity, the lust potion was working its special kind of magic. He knew that. He didn't pull away from her.

"You saved me," she whispered.

"Of course I did. I couldn't let you fall."

She laughed softly. "I think it's way too late for that."

"Emma—"

"I need you, Ryan. I want you. I don't care about anything else."

She was saying everything he wanted to hear, everything that made his heart swell so large it felt as if it might burst right out of his chest. Emma's voice, her scent—vanilla and roses—affected him like a drug. He was hard for her and the desire he heard in her words was matched by the desire he felt for her. "The lust potion, it's hard to ignore, I know...but..."

Then Emma kissed him and nothing else mattered.

9

THERE WAS NOTHING SHE WANTED more than this. More than Ryan. She didn't know why she'd tried to fight it so much before.

He was basically perfect—funny, sexy, warm. There was just that one little thing that kept her from giving in to her feelings for him.

His damn lies.

But everybody lied from time to time. She wasn't sure if it was worth worrying about as much as she always did. She worried too much for her own good.

Ryan tasted as amazing as he had the other night. It was a kiss that turned her liquid and hot inside. She knew he felt the same for her. She'd felt it earlier—his cock was thick and hard as it pressed almost painfully against her stomach. He wanted her.

Which was a very good thing, because she's never been this turned on in her entire life.

"You sure about this?" he whispered against her lips.

"About us being together in a dusty old hotel room?"

"Surprisingly not as dusty as I would have guessed."

"These rooms were sealed up pretty well."

"Obviously, this was meant to happen then." He kissed her again and his hands moved up to slide over her breasts. He groaned. "You are so gorgeous."

She laughed a little. "Sure, *now* you think it. When we were partners—"

"When we were partners I could barely keep my hands off of you. I've always wanted you, Em."

An unwelcome thought strayed too close to ignore. "What about Charlotte?"

"Charlotte asked me out. I said yes. I wanted you, but you were my partner and my friend and I didn't want to…" He shook his head. "I didn't want to mess that up. My relationships have never lasted all that long before. It was important to me not to jeopardize what we already had. Besides, partners aren't supposed to sleep together."

"Others have broken that rule."

"Now I know." His hands slid down to curl around the curve of her ass. "If you only knew how many cold showers I had to take when we worked together…"

She couldn't help but smile. He'd wanted her like she'd wanted him. It was what she'd always needed to hear.

The longer she touched him, that he touched her, the more out of control she felt. The more she needed to feel his skin against hers. "Forget about the past. I need you naked right now, Ryan."

He swore under his breath. "And then what do you need?"

She raised an eyebrow. "You want me to tell you?"

"You're the writer. Yeah, tell me, Em. Tell me what you want me to do to you."

An electric thrill went through her. "I never intended to become a writer. But I had so many fantasies—I had to get them down on paper. It just happened."

"It doesn't matter. It happened. So tell me what you want."

"You already read my book, so that's cheating. You know about my fantasies. Why don't you tell me what *you* want?"

His gaze burned into hers. "I want to take off your clothes slowly, one piece at a time. Then I need to see you naked and spread across that bed."

As he spoke the words, he unbuttoned her blouse carefully, although she noticed his hands were trembling. He peeled the silk off her shoulders and let it fall softly to the floor, leaving her standing there in a black satin push up bra and black skirt.

"Can I help?" she asked breathlessly.

He grinned. "I think I can handle it."

His hands moved to the small of her back and he slid the zipper down, then skimmed the skirt over her hips, letting it fall to the ground as well.

His gaze raked her, but he didn't touch her. Not yet. Her skin felt flushed.

"Now what?" she asked.

"Now…" He drew closer and slid a finger under the strap of her bra, pulling it down so just the pale pink edge of her nipple was exposed. His careful approach was driving her insane with the need to feel his hands on her. Her body ached to be touched, stroked, caressed. But Ryan seemed to be in no hurry as he turned his attention to the other strap, before reaching around to unhook the bra. It also fell to the floor.

Desire darkened his gaze. He leaned over and swept his tongue over her right nipple, cupping her left breast in his hand. An involuntary moan escaped her lips as he sucked on her aching nipples, and a surge of molten-hot lust shot directly to her sex. She felt a frantic need to have him between her legs.

Emma struggled to breathe. "You're not really giving a good narration of your intentions."

"Sometimes actions speak louder than words." He grinned at her, then directed her backward toward the bed. She sat down on the edge of it and looked up at him. "Lie back, Em."

She did as he asked. The bed felt soft and smelled clean, not musty. She inhaled sharply when Ryan sat down next to where she lay and slid his hand along her body, coming to rest just above her panties. He teased the elastic waist band and she squirmed against the bed spread, raising her hips up to meet his heated touch.

"I told you the Desidero potion was powerful stuff." His voice was raspy.

"It is." She couldn't think about much more than what his fingers were doing. "Touch me, Ryan."

"I am touching you."

She glared up at him. "You're not playing fair."

"I asked you to tell me what you wanted, but you didn't. So..."

"I can tell you."

"Then do so."

"Lower."

He raised an eyebrow. "Lower? Lower what?"

She grabbed hold of his hand and moved it down between her legs. The press of his fingers over her clit, even through a thin layer of fabric, was enough to make her arch up off the bed.

Ryan whispered in her ear. "Oh, Em. You're so damn hot you're going to burn me. But I want closer to the flame."

She almost smiled, but the expression was difficult to

pull off when waves of pleasure were washing over her. "Listen to you. I knew you had a literary bone in your body."

But she stopped talking, stopped thinking, when he slid his hand under the edge of fabric to slide against the slickness of her sex without any barriers between them.

"Oh, Ryan...yes—" Although it showed an utter lack of control on her part, she couldn't help it. Only a few brushes of his fingers against her were enough to make her raggedly cry out his name as the waves of her orgasm crashed over her.

It seemed to be enough to shatter his control as well.

He pulled her panties off, leaving her completely naked before him. He got to his knees on the bed and undid his shirt without taking his gaze away from her.

"What do you want, Em?" he asked, an edge of desperation in his words, almost as if he was fighting to maintain control over himself.

The thought excited her.

"You," she breathed. "I want you."

"Specific. Be specific."

"I want you inside of me."

"What inside of you?"

"Your cock."

"Emma...more..."

She glared at him, frustrated that he was making her talk instead of feel. Intense lust clouded her mind. "I want to feel your cock sliding in and out of me."

His expression darkened. "That's more like it."

"I...can't wait, Ryan. Please...the potion..." Her skin felt like it was on fire. She reached for him, sliding her hands over his chest and down over the hard ridges of his abdomen. That he was still dressed and she was naked made her feel wanton and seductive.

"Is it only the potion, Em?" he whispered.

She stroked his erection that tented his jeans before unbuttoning and unzipping him, pulling his jeans down over his hips so his cock stood out hard and long. She remembered how foggy her head had felt when she'd knelt in front of him in Xavier Franklin's library and taken him in her mouth. She'd been running on pure adrenalin and lust, not stopping long enough to give her actions much thought.

Tonight she felt more in control of her body, of her needs. The potion's effects were still driving her more than they might another night, swept away as she was by the need she felt for this beautiful man who drove her crazy in more ways than one, but she sensed that they were just amplifying a need that was already there, waiting. After all, she'd always wanted him, since the first moment she'd seen him. It had been only a fantasy then.

But this was no fantasy. It wasn't a chapter out of her book. This was real. Every sense she had—not including the sixth one—was focused entirely on Ryan, how good he smelled, tasted and felt, the sound of his moan as she wrapped her fingers around his length and began to stroke him. Knowing that he wanted her as much as she wanted him was so exciting. It made her happy, as if a small inner light that she hadn't been aware of, one which had been dark ever since Ryan had left Mystic Ridge, had been turned back on. Like the lights in the hotel that had flickered when Harold was here…Emma's inner light had been struggling to stay on. She just hadn't known why.

It was because she'd missed Ryan. She wanted him, she needed him, she…

She felt so much more than that. But that room was still dark and scary and she wasn't quite ready to shine the light on any deeper emotions just yet.

"Did you ask me a question?" she asked.

"I…" His forehead was creased. "I'm finding it very difficult to think straight at the moment."

"It's just a little lust. We have to give in to it," she said without releasing her hold on him. His chest was bare, with slabs of muscle. She knew he worked out at the gym. It showed. There wasn't an ounce of fat on him.

"Is that all this is?" he asked.

She watched him carefully. "Does there need to be more?"

His gaze sought hers. "I don't know."

"I don't want to think about anything other than this moment, okay? I don't want anything to ruin this."

A smile played at his lips. "As you wish." Then he squeezed his eyes shut as she continued to touch him. "Em, you're driving me crazy."

He wrapped his hand around her wrist and pulled her away from him, then kicked his jeans off the rest of the way. Pushing her back onto the bed, he trapped her wrists with one of his hands and moved them above her head so she was stretched out naked on the bed for him just as he wanted.

It was dark in the room, the full moon outside the window bathing them in silver and shadows.

"So beautiful," he whispered. His hand slid down her body, skimming her breasts, her stomach, until he was stroking her between her legs, the slick folds of her sex. Her breath came in short gasps and her legs unconsciously parted wider for him. "If you knew how many times I'd dreamed about this…"

She moaned as he slid his index finger inside of her, and slowly began pumping it in and out before adding a second finger.

"Ryan—" His name escaped from her throat, hoarse and filled with need. "Please, I want you…"

He brought his mouth down to brush against her ear. "Are you going to admit that the hero of your novel is based on me?"

The rapid movement of his fingers made it hard for her to concentrate on anything but pure sensation. He moved faster and deeper and another orgasm skittered just at the edge of her control.

She struggled to breathe normally. "Ryan…"

"Tell me, Em." There was a raw edge to his voice. "Tell me that I'm not the only one who's fantasized about this. About you. Tell me that you've wanted me, that you've missed me, that you never stopped aching for me."

"Yes," she moaned. "It's true. I want you. I've always wanted you, Ryan."

She felt him press his weight down on top of her, brushing his thick erection against her swollen sex. Just the feel of his cock against her clit was enough to make her climax again. She cried out and grabbed his shoulders, arching up against him.

He swore gutturally. "Too much… I can't wait…"

He reached over the side of the bed, grabbed his jeans, rooted in his wallet and pulled out a condom, which he tore open with his teeth and quickly sheathed himself with. The next moment she felt the tip of his erection push against her.

"I wanted to do this slowly, but I don't think that's going to be possible…" His voice trailed off.

She captured his face between her hands, kissing him with every ounce of passion she felt for him. "Slow, not necessary. Fast is good. Very good."

He grinned, but it looked labored. "I need you so badly…"

Emma leaned back onto the bed again, her hands digging into his bare hips as he settled between her thighs. He fought for some sort of control. Maybe on another day he'd win that battle, but with the lust potion working against him, he had no chance.

She gasped as he filled her completely with one deep thrust, her fingernails biting into his back. He didn't move. He just lay there on top of her, sheathed inside of her as she got used to the aching pleasure of feeling him stretching her body to accommodate his length and width.

"Emma…" he whispered, then inhaled sharply. "You feel so good."

She almost smiled at him using her full name. She liked how it sounded on his lips, half hidden by the dark lust in his voice.

"It's better," she whispered after he brushed his lips against hers.

He looked down at her, frowning. "What is?"

"This. It's better than my book. Better than my fantasies. You…inside me…it's better than I ever could have imagined."

"Damn." His frown deepened. "And here I was trying not to completely lose my mind. You're not making it very easy for me."

He kissed her, hard and deep and hot and wet, and his

hips began to move against hers. The slow, deep thrust of his cock inside of her commanded all of her attention, all of her emotion. There wasn't time to think about anything else, worry about anything else.

Was it only because of a lust potion? She'd wanted him, she'd always wanted him, but this irresistible pull she felt toward Ryan that brought them together tonight, in a formerly haunted hotel…would she have even been here if it hadn't been for the potion?

No. She would have avoided him. Avoided this. And Ryan wouldn't have returned to Mystic Ridge to see her again. It was the potion to blame. It was the potion to thank.

Ryan felt so good, he fit her perfectly. He was made to make love to her, like this. Here. Now. It was inevitable.

As his thrusts became quicker, deeper, faster, her thoughts again grew cloudy. The heat of his skin, his chest and hands and mouth and tongue sliding against her were all she could focus on. His taste—salty, warm and wet. The slide of his cock inside her.

He pulled her up off the bed, gathering her in his arms, her legs wrapping around his waist. "Emma—"

She just held on, lost in sensation. Lost in Ryan.

He kissed her hard, deep, his tongue tangling with hers. Then he broke the kiss, dug his fingers into her ass and thrust up hard and deep, a dark, guttural cry of her name on his lips as his climax quaked through him.

Ryan collapsed on top of her, a raspy laugh at the back of his throat. She threaded her fingers in his hair as his arms came around her. He hugged her tight against his chest.

"So…" he said after a moment.

She smiled. "So."

"How much do you suppose they charge for a night in this dump?"

"I've heard their rates are quite reasonable. Two hair pins per night."

He propped himself up on his elbow, his right hand leisurely exploring Emma's back. "I think I just saw a dust bunny. It poked its head out from behind the closet door."

When Emma had left for her date with Leo tonight, the last place she thought she'd end up was in a previously haunted hotel room with Ryan. "So what happens now?"

"Now?"

"We consummated our...uh, lust. That mean the Desidero potion will start fading quicker now, right?"

He grinned. "You did some research."

"A little. But I'll save the true expertise for you and Professor Snape."

"Once the lust is given in to, then the effects will begin to dissipate. They would have departed anyway, in about a week. But now...it shouldn't take all that long at all until we're back to normal."

"And then, what? We'll go back to feeling just strong friendship for each other?"

"I doubt it. I've never felt only friendship for you, Em."

She raised an eyebrow. "And now that you've tasted the forbidden fruit?"

"I'm seriously considering becoming a fruitarian." He smiled and brushed his lips over her right nipple before flicking it with the tip of his tongue, making her gasp. "That's a vegetarian who only eats fruit, I think. *Forbidden* fruit."

She laughed and fresh desire for him slid through her.

He drew back up to her face and kissed her lips. "I want to make love to you all night long."

"Let's go back to my place."

"Yeah?"

She just nodded. "Fewer dust bunnies, I promise. And a much more comfortable bed."

"You know the way to my heart." He groaned when she took hold of his rapidly stiffening cock and began to stroke it. "So if you want to leave, what do you think you're doing, Ms. Black?"

"One for the road." She leaned over to grab another condom out of his wallet on the bedside table, opened it up and rolled it on him. Then she rose up on the bed, straddled his body so she hovered over the tip of his cock, and then lowered herself down on him, taking him inside of her an inch at a time.

"No self-control at all," he whispered. "So shocking."

She grinned. "I know. I still blame it on the potion."

He cupped her buttocks as she slid up and down on his length. Conversation was at an end, there was only the sensation of his body moving inside of hers. She was living every one of her fantasies about Ryan, one by one. She'd only started at the top of the list. There were many more to go. This is what she'd always wanted.

Part of her remembered that Ryan wasn't perfect, that he wasn't going to be in her life for much longer. There was no way she could totally forgive him for what he'd done, what he refused to admit. While this was wonderful, amazing, this chance to touch him, to feel him, to make love to him—it didn't change anything.

Emma wanted him. A large part of her knew she was falling even deeper in love with him than she already had, but still another part knew she had to break that fall before it was too late.

She'd have this perfect hour or two with him here. Then at her house. It would be sex like she'd never experienced it before—mind-blowing and the culmination of all of her fantasies. But it couldn't be real. Tomorrow things would be different.

As much as she was beginning to wish otherwise....

10

EMMA WAS INSATIABLE. They made love twice in the hotel room, and again at her house. Ryan had taken her deep and hard and fast, then slower and sweeter. For a moment, she'd looked up at him as he moved inside her, her body clenching his, her mouth seeking his to kiss, that he was certain she would whisper that she loved him.

But she hadn't.

Ryan hadn't slept around much since he'd left Mystic Ridge. He wasn't a monk so there had been a couple of women—both one-night stands. Both times they'd been redheads.

He knew he had it bad for Emma—he'd known it for a while. But actually being with her had done him in for good.

Still, there was a little piece of herself that she was holding back from him and it was driving him crazy.

She didn't ask him to leave, so he stayed by her side, sleeping in her bed, her body warm and soft and sexy curved against his. He could definitely get used to this.

"Was it really better?" he whispered to her.

She turned around so they were face-to-face. "Better?"

"You said you and me... That it was better than your

fantasies. Better than your book." He laughed under his breath. "This is me being needy."

She smiled, a sweet, shy smile that betrayed how open and sexy she'd been only a short time ago. He still felt the lust potion swirling between them, threatening to cloud his thoughts, driving him to make love to her again instead of wasting time talking. But talking with Emma wasn't wasted time.

She brushed her mouth against his. "Did you really read it? All the way through?"

He grinned and traced a line on her plump bottom lip. "Yes. Twice."

"Twice?"

"I never knew I was such a bookworm."

"I'm a little embarrassed. I'm not the best writer in the world."

"You're amazing," he assured her. "For real. There was only one bad thing about the book."

"Which was?"

"Nobody lived happily ever after."

Her cautious look turned amused. "A sucker for a Hollywood ending, are you?"

"Again, it's news to me. But I guess I am."

"It was a journey for my heroine. She needed to experience life in all its facets before she truly understood herself."

"And she left the hero behind when she moved away. I thought they were in love."

"They might hook up again. Someday." She shrugged a bare shoulder and he slid his hand over it, fascinated by every move she made.

"You didn't answer my question. Does this—what happened between us tonight—really compare to your fantasies?"

"My novel was only fiction." She traced her fingers over the stubble on his jaw. "This was real."

"Was it?" He searched her face.

She bit her bottom lip. "It felt pretty damn real to me. Lust potions notwithstanding."

"Is that a good thing?"

"Ryan Shephard, you really *are* needy."

"I seem to have gotten that way recently. I…I just want to make sure you don't regret what happened between us."

She studied his face for a moment. "It doesn't change anything. It doesn't change…what happened before."

Even though he'd never felt so good, his body pressed against the warmth of Emma's, her words cut him like a knife slicing through his heart. He'd forgotten how dangerous she could be when he let his guard down. "What do I have to do…to *say*…to make you believe that I had nothing to do with that? I'm innocent, Emma. One hundred percent."

A shadow crossed her face and she frowned, finally breaking their eye contact. "Let's not talk about it."

His heart felt like a thick lump of coal in his chest. "I wish you could believe me. What I told you I did as a teenager…it means nothing. I'm different now. If you can't believe me, then I don't know if anyone ever will."

"Why can't you just admit it?" she asked quietly, her voice breaking.

He stroked her hair back from her face. "Maybe you're right."

Her glossy eyes widened. "I am?"

"Yeah. Let's just forget it."

He turned over and dug his fingers into the pillow. It took a long time before he finally fell asleep.

When Ryan woke in the morning, Emma was snuggled up next to him. He pulled her closer and kissed her. She kissed him back, but there was something in the kiss that made it feel just a little less urgent than it had been last night.

When she slipped out of the bed and went to the bathroom to shower, she didn't invite him along. He tried not to take it personally.

She wanted him and he knew that a part of her did care for him, but there was a wall there. It didn't take too much thought to figure out what that wall was built from—her being convinced that he was a thief and a liar.

Damn it. What did he have to do to prove he wasn't guilty? There had been security camera footage, but it wasn't conclusive. He'd seen it. It could have been anyone with dark hair, around six feet tall and male. It was grainy and the camera never got a clear shot of the thief's face.

But there had been a witness. Only that witness had lied. He just damn well wished he knew who it was because he'd demand to know why they wanted to ruin his life.

And he wished that Emma would take him at his word. He wasn't sure what he'd ever done to give her reason to doubt him so much. What someone did when they were a stupid teenager shouldn't be held against him for the rest of his life.

Ryan showered quickly after Emma exited the small bathroom, then got dressed.

"Emma...we need to talk." He leaned against the wall in her kitchen where he'd found her eating a bowl of cereal.

She glanced at her watch. "I really need to get to the office."

"Can't that wait?"

"No." She bit her bottom lip again before meeting his gaze.

"Don't tell me you wish last night hadn't happened."

"I'm not saying that." She swallowed hard.

"Then what are you saying?"

"I wish things were different, Ryan."

"They can be."

She looked distraught.

There was a knock on the front door and Emma went toward it, opening it up.

"Thought I'd swing by and see if you wanted to grab coffee before we go to the office," Charlotte's voice rang out. "And I wanted to see how your date with Leo went last…" She trailed off. "Oh, my God. Ryan?"

He forced himself to look toward the door where the beautiful blonde glanced in at him. He was surprised she hadn't been here when they'd returned last night. She and Emma used to be roommates. Emma always treated her like a little sister who needed guidance and support after she'd left the support of her previously wealthy family to branch out on her own. "Charlotte. What's new?"

"I…" Charlotte's confused gaze snapped to Emma, then back at him. "Long time no see."

"Yes, it is, isn't it?"

"Everything okay here, Emma?" she asked tightly.

Ryan repressed a humorless laugh. Not much of a greeting from a woman he'd dated. It just went to show that she had found their relationship to be about as serious as he had. In other words, not very.

Charlotte had been fun—a laugh, a distraction, and she'd seemed into him, but there hadn't been any more to it than that. He'd realized that after they'd been together a month. It was a surface relationship only, nothing too deep. He'd dated her mainly to help him keep from pursuing Emma, something that would have jeopardized their friendship. If the shit hadn't hit the fan with the burglary pinned on him, he didn't think his relationship with Charlotte would have lasted much longer. And then he'd have been free to see if he and Emma shared more than friendship.

"Yeah," Emma said after an uncomfortable moment of silence passed between them. "Everything's fine."

"If you say so." Charlotte cleared her throat. "I should...go. I'll, uh, catch up with you at the office, okay?"

"Charlotte—" Emma called.

"Bye." Charlotte left through the door. Ryan thought for a moment that Emma would go after her but she stayed in place.

"Wow," he said after another moment passed. "It's great that we can all still be friends."

Emma's expression grew tense. "Look, Ryan, I need to go. I'll see you later?"

That thick wall she had up between them again was starting to piss him off. He didn't want there to be anything between them and yet that barrier stood there, a hundred feet in the air. He'd have talked to her about it, but it would have to be later.

"Dinner?" he asked. "I'll pick you up after work?"

She nodded. "Okay."

"The lust potion..." he said, his voice trailing off.

"I still feel it," she said. "Strongly."

"When it fades..."

"Let's cross that bridge when we come to it."

He wanted to cross a lot of bridges with Emma if he

was given the chance. However, it seemed as if the tolls he had to pay to cross them were well out of his price range.

He wanted to kiss her goodbye, but he didn't. He left, got in his car—his prized '68 Mustang GT-390 that had been both a vehicle and a home to him on more nights than he'd like to admit lately—and drove to the motel where he was staying. He'd had a rented apartment when he'd lived here before, but he'd let that go and had been living out of suitcases in several towns ever since, picking up a bit of work at garages here and there.

Out of his rearview mirror he could tell that he was being followed.

"Fantastic," he said dryly. He peered at the reflection again to see that it was Charlotte driving a silver Lexus coupe with its top down. Tailing him like he was a criminal and she was an FBI agent.

He didn't bother pulling over, since he wanted to see if she'd keep following him. She did, all the way to his motel. She parked next to him, then got out of the car and slammed the door. It seemed as if she was going to tell him off, yell at him to stay the hell away from Emma, just as a proper protective "little sister" would do. The usual runaround.

He eyed her as she approached him. "Okay, Charlotte, let's have it."

"It's been a long time, Ryan," she said.

"It has been. So what do you—?"

She threw herself at him and kissed him hard on the mouth, her tongue seeking his, her fingernails raking down his back. When she stepped back, she was breathless. "Damn, I've missed you."

"Whoa, wait a minute." He grabbed her arms and pushed her away from him. "What the hell is this?"

She grinned wickedly. "It's me playing hooky from work so we can reacquaint ourselves with each other. I don't share that house with Emma anymore. I'm assuming you were there looking for me."

"Charlotte—"

"I've fantasized about this, Ryan. My body has missed yours."

He eyed her. "Yeah? That's a little hard to believe considering I haven't heard one word from you in six months."

"I wanted things to cool off first. But it's not like I haven't thought about you." She moved toward him but he stepped out of her reach.

"Things have cooled off," he said. "If you mean between you and me."

"I was talking about the robbery, actually." Understanding slid behind her gaze. "If you're not here to see me again, then what are you doing back in Mystic Ridge?"

"I wanted to see Emma."

Her eyes widened. *"Emma."*

"Yeah." Emma had always extended herself way too much with Charlotte, Ryan thought. She'd let herself be used a bit, under the guise of friendship. Women could be wily when they wanted something. Charlotte hadn't had much in the way of savings when she came to town and took the job with PARA. Emma had offered to share her house until Charlotte got on her feet. She'd been a sounding board and a true friend.

Not to say that Charlotte was that bad, but he'd always worried that Emma felt their friendship was stronger than it really was. People who wanted something could be very convincing.

Charlotte swept a glance over the length of him. "I

always had a feeling you were interested in her. Even when we were together."

"You're so perceptive. Then again, you are an empath just like me."

"No, not just like you, Ryan. My abilities are much stronger."

She'd sent that out to wound, but it didn't hit the mark. "What we had is long over, Charlotte. I can't imagine you really give that much of a shit. I heard you're dating Stephen now."

"I am."

"More power to you. I'll refrain from letting him know about this. I'm sure it was a little slip-up that won't be repeated and that you're one hundred percent faithful to my old friend."

She twisted a finger into her long blond hair. "We have an open relationship."

"Then there's no problem."

Charlotte shook her head as she studied him. "You and Emma, huh? Is it something real between the two of you?"

Admitting that out loud would mean that he thought that they had a chance. "Maybe."

He braced himself for her reaction and thought for a moment she'd be angry. Instead she nodded. "She's a great catch. She's never been anything but wonderful to me."

"I know. On both counts."

She wiped at her mouth where her lipstick had smeared from kissing him. "After everything that happened before, I have to say I'm a bit surprised she's open to having you back in her life."

"I'm innocent," he said simply, pushing away the stab

of annoyance at being reminded, yet again, that everyone in the universe seemed to think he was a thief.

"If you say so." She shook her head.

"I do. It's true. And it's only a matter of time before Emma realizes that. Before everyone realizes it."

She frowned. "I just can't believe it."

"Believe what? That she'd give me half a chance, despite everything that's been said about me? I worked with her. She was my friend. She's still my friend, even though she's having trouble accepting my innocence in this ridiculous matter."

Charlotte's lips thinned. "Well, of course she's having trouble. Do you blame her?"

He stared at her. "What are you talking about?"

She looked at him incredulously. "Don't you even know? Emma's the one who confirmed to Patrick that it was you in the first place. Of course she wouldn't believe anything else."

Ryan just stared at her for a long moment of silence, not quite believing what he'd just heard. "Excuse me?"

She looked confused as she shrugged. "Emma says she saw you that night, Ryan. She watched you leave the building with the stolen merchandise in hand. The video wouldn't have been enough on its own, but with her word... Well, Emma's the most honest person I've ever known in my life. She tells it like it is, which is why Patrick believed her without any argument. She wouldn't sell out her own partner just for shits and giggles. It was devastating for her."

Emma was the one who'd gotten him fired. She was the one who told the agency manager that Ryan was the thief.

Why would she do that? Why would she ruin his life like that? It didn't make any sense.

"Great seeing you again, Charlotte," Ryan said through gritted teeth. "But I have things to do. Give my regards to Stephen."

He turned and went to his motel-room door, let himself in and closed it behind him, leaving him standing alone in the dark room.

"Emma's the most honest person I've ever known in my life."

Charlotte didn't know how wrong she was about that.

Emma had lied. Blatantly.

Emma got him fired. He had no damn idea why she'd set him up, but he was going to find out. And she was damn well going to tell him the truth.

11

THANK GOD IT WAS FRIDAY. Today seemed to consist entirely of paperwork. It wasn't Emma's favorite job by a long shot. No, she preferred doing field work—showing up at a place and investigating first-hand. But she didn't get to do that much since she was currently between partners.

She'd checked in with the potions department to make sure the Desidero potion was being kept under lock and key. It was. And they'd already determined that it was a viable potion—not that that was news to Emma. They had a dozen other potions on hand that were of varying degrees of volatility—lust and love potions, potions that make one disappear, potions that changed a person's hair color or length of one's nose. There was even a potion that helped someone speak a different language. Unfortunately, it only covered Latin. Not all that useful in everyday life.

There weren't any potions to solve her current problems, though. Not unless she wanted to take something to make her forget everything.

No thanks.

Memories of last night also accompanied her to work, and the dull paper pushing only made her focus more on what had happened between her and Ryan.

She'd given in to her lust for him. And it had been incredible.

More than that. She'd felt more, so much more. It scared her how much she liked spending time with him. Figuring out Harold's problem with Ryan at her side only made her remember how good they'd been as partners.

Just as she'd hoped, Patrick had been very impressed that she'd solved the Maison Duchamp case. Mission accomplished.

However, it scared her to think about how much she missed Ryan, even after just a few hours. She counted down the hours, the minutes, until the workday was over and he'd pick her up for dinner like he promised. In the meantime, she couldn't figure out why Charlotte hadn't come to see her to find out why Ryan had been at her house this morning.

Emma finally approached her close to five o'clock and stood by her desk until Charlotte looked up from her computer monitor where she was doing the monthly categorization of a long list of potions, as well as items currently being held in the vault—a tedious job Emma had been saddled with many times before.

"What's up?" Charlotte said when she noticed Emma lurking nearby.

"Are you mad at me?"

Charlotte pushed back from her desk and swiveled around in her chair to regard Emma. "Why would you think something like that?"

"You've been ignoring me all day."

"I haven't been ignoring you. I've just been really busy."

"Look, I know that you and Ryan used to date." Emma leaned against the side of Charlotte's desk. "I can see why you might be mad about finding him there with me this morning."

"I'm not mad."

Emma raked a hand through her hair, sweeping it all over her right shoulder. "You're dating Stephen now. I don't see why you'd have a problem with me and Ryan."

Charlotte pushed back from her desk and stood up. "If I have a problem, it's not because of me. It's because of you. Emma, honey, I'm not jealous, I'm worried about you."

That was much worse, actually. "Don't worry about me. Ryan's a good man."

"Uh, actually, no, he isn't. He's a thief. A liar." She counted the points off on her fingertips. "If I'd wanted to date somebody like him, now that we know what he's capable of, you definitely would have warned me off. So let me do the same in return. Think, Emma. He's probably come back to Mystic Ridge so he can break into the vault again." She glanced at her list. "There is some choice merchandise in there right now. Big-ticket stuff."

Emma didn't want to think that could possibly be the reason. There was no way Ryan would come within a hundred feet of the vault—he knew the consequences would be much worse than simply losing his job.

"Just forget I said anything. I'll talk to you later, okay?" Emma felt more tense than she'd been all day as she walked away from Charlotte's desk. It was time to leave. Ryan was likely already waiting for her.

"This isn't a chapter from your book, Emma," Charlotte called after her. "He's not a romantic hero who only wants to sweep you off your feet. Trust me, I know that first-hand."

She froze. A few months ago she'd confided to Charlotte her secret about her writing—how she'd been getting her fantasies out on paper. She just hadn't let on who the inspiration was behind those fantasies. She'd even given Charlotte a copy of the book when she'd received a bunch in the mail last week. "I don't think that."

Charlotte approached her and put a hand on her shoulder. "I know he's hard to resist. But don't confuse a sexy smile and a fantastic body with something real. There are better men out there for you. Trust me on that."

"Don't worry." Emma forced a pleasant expression to her face. "It's all good. A fling to get him out of my system once and for all means absolutely nothing in the long run."

"Well, that's good to hear. Besides, that Leo guy is way better for you. He owns his own business, right? What does Ryan have to offer you? Nothing but heartache."

Emma left the office with Charlotte's words echoing in her ears and a churning in her gut. Just as she'd expected, Ryan was waiting for her in the parking lot. She got in the passenger side of his Mustang and let out a very long, shaky breath.

"You okay?" he asked.

"Yeah, fine. Sorry, it's just been kind of a tough day."

"For you and me both."

Ryan looked good. She liked that he didn't wear suits

all the time like some of the men she'd dated in the past. Ryan was casual both in clothing and attitude. He wore black jeans today and a dark blue shirt, unbuttoned at the throat. His hair looked as unruly as it had when they'd first woken up that morning. It was a good, sexy look for him. He wasn't totally casual today, though. He also seemed a bit tense. She couldn't really blame him. Being back in Mystic Ridge must be difficult for him.

It was also difficult for Emma on levels she never would have guessed. The two sides of herself fought against each other—one wanting to kiss him, make love to him again; the other wanting answers to difficult questions.

"So, where are we going?" She couldn't say she was all that hungry for dinner, but spending time with Ryan— even after her exchange with Charlotte—was not an unpleasant thought. She could put their issues out of her head for a couple of hours and try to enjoy what they had between them for a little while longer.

"I have somewhere perfect in mind." He pulled away from the curb.

After ten minutes, he drove off the main road and turned into a small secluded park where Emma knew families came for barbecues and long walks in nature. It also had the reputation of being the go-to place for local teenagers Friday and Saturday nights if they wanted to park their cars and make out.

Her brows went up. "I thought we were headed to a restaurant. Are we having a picnic instead? Based on my footwear, you should know I'm not really the outdoorsy type."

"No picnic. I wanted to come somewhere private so we could talk." He still had his hands tight on the steering wheel and was looking straight forward. "I think I need some air."

He got out of the car and paced toward the front of it, sitting down on the hood with his back toward Emma.

She exited the car a few moments later and drew closer to him. He finally glanced at her, and shook his head, his expression troubled.

"What?" she asked.

"I don't know why I'm still here. I just came to Mystic Ridge to return your books and potion bottle. I didn't mean to stay this long."

He looked seriously upset. Concern swelled inside of her.

"Something's wrong," she said. "Tell me what it is."

He stood up and moved closer to her so he was only a foot away. He studied her face so intently she wondered if there was going to be a test later. "I just don't get it, Em."

"Get what?"

"You say I'm the liar, but…it just doesn't make any sense to me."

She eyed him warily. "Have you been drinking?"

"No. Not yet. Although it's definitely been penciled in for later." He frowned deeply. "Do you feel anything for me, beyond what the lust potion inspired? Do you care about me at all?"

That was blunt. So blunt that she took a step back from him, her breath catching in her chest. "That was unexpected."

"I don't have time to play games."

Emma exhaled shakily. "I don't know what I'm feeling, to tell you the truth."

He snorted without any humor and braced a hand

against the passenger-side window. "Interesting choice of words. *To tell you the truth.*"

She didn't need to be psychic to sense this wasn't going to be a pleasant evening with a nice candlelit dinner. Ryan was agitated and it seemed to be directed toward Emma herself.

"Maybe we should do this some other time, Ryan," she said after a moment. "I don't know what's up with you right now, but I think you should take me back to my car now."

Being near Ryan was confusing enough, but with the Desidero potion's effects still swirling around her, especially when he was this close, it made it difficult for her to think properly. She wanted him, she needed him, but she couldn't figure him out. Ryan Shephard was an enigma to her and that just made everything more difficult.

Emma wanted her life to be simple again.

But wanting Ryan this badly made it anything but.

RYAN WAS SO CLOSE TO figuring out why his life had imploded six months ago that he couldn't let this night simply end with no solid answers. It was time to get everything out on the table and see how Emma responded. He couldn't let his emotions get the better of him, even if his desire for the woman standing in front of him right now was proving to be a distraction.

"I know what you did, Em," he said.

There. That was a good start.

Her shoulders stiffened. "Excuse me?"

"You heard me." He squeezed his eyes shut for a moment to regain his resolve and then opened them to face the woman who'd singlehandedly destroyed his life.

He never thought such a deception would cut him so deeply.

She frowned. "What do you mean, you know what I did?"

He watched her closely, waiting to gauge her reaction to what he was about to say. "Charlotte told me the truth this morning. I don't know why you didn't say anything to me. It would have made everything so much simpler."

She looked confused. "The truth about what?"

"About the robbery that night at PARA. The one that *you* witnessed. It was *you*, Emma. You're the one who pointed the finger at me and got me fired."

Her face paled and she twisted the handle of her purse between her hands. "It wasn't Charlotte's place to say anything."

So it *was* true. There had still been a glimmer of hope inside him that Charlotte had been lying, but Emma had just confirmed it. "You don't think I have the right to know who my accuser was?"

Emma raised her green-eyed gaze to his, her thin, arched eyebrows, much darker than the flame red of her long hair, drawn together. "I didn't want it to be more difficult between us than it already was."

His throat felt tight. "I just don't understand. Why would you do that to me?"

Her confused expression intensified. "Why would I do that to you?"

"Yes."

"I don't understand. What would you have wanted me to do? Lie for you? Be your cover, or something? I don't know if I could have lived with myself if I'd lied to Patrick."

Ryan grew more confused with every moment that passed. "But you didn't see me. You couldn't have."

She pulled her hair over her right shoulder and twisted a strand with her index finger. Her beautiful face had grown weary and sad. "But I *did* see you. I'm sorry, Ryan, but I did. I wish so hard that it wasn't true, but…" She exhaled shakily and looked up into his eyes. "I don't want you to be hurt over this anymore. I can see for myself that you're not one of the bad guys. Whatever drove you to steal that night…whatever demons you were dealing with, I can help you come back from that. I'm so sorry I turned my back on you—it won't happen again. But first you have to admit what you did once and for all. Will you do that for me?"

Ryan just stared at her for a long moment in silence as her words sank in. He'd expected her to deny it, to point the finger at Charlotte or somebody else as being the real tattler. But she wasn't doing that. She was owning up to the fact that she'd been the one to tell on him.

It was clear in her eyes she believed she was telling the truth. Emma thought she saw him steal that night, otherwise she never would have made up this story. She had nothing to gain from it.

Which made absolutely no goddamned sense at all. Because he hadn't stolen anything.

So if neither of them was lying…they had a big problem.

He reached for her hand and she didn't try to pull away from him. He didn't need the contact to tap into his empathic ability. He knew she was telling the truth.

Emma looked up at him with a very serious expression. "Are you going to say anything?"

"I'm just trying to figure everything out."

"What's there to figure out?"

"You really do want to help me, don't you?"

"Of course I do."

"Why?"

She pulled her hand away from his and pressed back against the side of the car, averting her gaze. "Because I care about you, Ryan. I know we all have our crosses to bear. You said you had a lousy childhood and that your brother got you into some trouble growing up, things you never would have done without his influence."

"True. But he's changed since then and so have I."

"And I know your psychic ability is a bit underdeveloped, but I never thought it held you back at all. You have a way with people. You can see the truth if you concentrate hard enough."

Emma knew him, he couldn't deny it. The tight knot in his gut finally loosened. He had a hard time believing he'd ever doubted her in the first place. The woman was one hundred percent genuine. What you saw was what you got with Emma Black.

He raked a hand through his hair. "Well, I do wish I could admit everything to you, Em. I really do. I honestly don't blame you for telling Patrick what you saw that night."

She looked shocked at this. "You don't?"

"No. I wouldn't expect anyone to jeopardize their own jobs on my account. You did the right thing. But there's just one really big problem with everything you've told me tonight."

"And what's that?"

He came closer so he could lean over and whisper into her ear. "I didn't do it."

The sentence was clear, blunt, and he waited for her

reaction. The wall started to come down over her expression when a moment ago it had been completely transparent. She began to move away from him but he grabbed her by her upper arms. His heart pounded hard in his chest, causing lust and something hotter and even sweeter to course through him.

He crushed his mouth against hers, kissing her hard and deep. It only took a moment before she kissed him back just as passionately, sliding her hands down his chest, before she braced herself against him and pushed back a couple of inches.

There was desire and confusion in her gaze.

Ryan shook his head. "I know what it sounds like, that I'm in denial."

"Big-time denial." She sounded breathless.

"Just hear me out, Em. I brought you here tonight to confront you, to make you admit that you'd lied about what you saw."

"But—"

He cut her off. "But you *weren't* lying. You *did* see me. Which leaves me with a really big problem because I didn't do it. Whoever you saw that night wasn't me."

He'd been so furious with her only a few minutes ago, but now he was confused...and more relieved than he thought possible.

Emma frowned hard. "That doesn't make any sense. I saw you. What, do you have a twin walking around town, or something?"

"I don't have a twin."

"Then how?" She paced across the parking lot and then came back, her expression tense with concentration.

"I don't know." He wracked his brain for the answer.

"Wait." Her brows were drawn together. "It wasn't you, but it was someone who looked like you."

"Yes."

"But I saw him. He looked…" She searched his face. "He looked exactly like you. What could make that possible? I wasn't hypnotized. I wasn't influenced. Nobody even knew I was there. But…" Her eyes widened.

"What is it?"

"You—you said you know potions, right? More than just the Desidero one?"

"Yeah." He raced to catch up with her line of thinking. "When I started at PARA, Patrick recognized that my psychic ability wasn't one hundred percent, so he had me do some extra work in the potions department as a backup. It would give me a little extra expertise to help pad out my résumé."

"When I dropped off the Desidero bottle yesterday, I saw some of the other ones we have in the office. It's amazing what some of them can do. Some change your hair color, your eye color, make you more beautiful or uglier…although, not sure why anyone would want that. But—but is there one that might make you look like somebody else entirely?"

His eyes widened as it all began to click for him. "Super rare and very old. Goes by the nickname Doppelganger. If you mix this potion with the blood or hair of your victim you'll temporarily appear to others as that person. And PARA had a small amount of it in the potions department. I remember seeing it on the list once."

Emma's faced paled. "You can't be serious."

"DNA is what helps it do its hocus pocus. The effects last only a couple hours."

Even though Emma herself had brought up the subject, she looked as if she was fighting this new possibility. "So someone could have used this potion so they could look like you when they stole from the vault?"

It didn't exactly sound like a story that would hold up in court, but he nodded firmly. "That's it. That has to be it. There's no other explanation."

She swallowed hard. "I don't know. I don't know if I really believe it. It's too far-fetched."

"Then that's the question, isn't it? You either believe this crazy explanation or you continue to believe that I'm a scumbag who enjoys lying to your face. I don't have a lot of time here to wait for your decision, though. I need to get back to New York as soon as possible."

She exhaled shakily. "What's in New York?"

"Xavier Franklin and his priceless collection of glassware. I'm positive he's bought one of the stolen pieces from whomever the real thief was. That's the reason I was there the other night." He crossed his arms over his chest. "So what'll it be, Em? Believe that the Doppelganger potion's the thing to blame, or that I'm a big liar who doesn't deserve to be anywhere near you."

Emma stared at him, her face pale, her brow creased. "This is crazy, Ryan. Just because I believe in lust potions doesn't mean I believe in one like this. I don't know much about potions."

"But I do, so you need to trust *me*." He stood there another minute as silence stretched between them. His chest tightened with disappointment and he nodded with a firm shake of his head. "Come on. I should probably take you home now."

He turned away from her and moved around to the

driver's side of the car. He opened the door, his heart feeling very heavy.

"Wait!"

He heard the clip clop of her high heels on the pavement of the small deserted parking lot and he glanced over his shoulder to see her swiftly moving toward him.

"It's okay, Em. Really—"

She grabbed hold of him, throwing her arms around his shoulders, and pulling his face down to hers so she could kiss him hard and passionately on the mouth. He gasped against her lips in surprise.

"What are you doing?" he asked.

She was smiling and shaking her head. "This is me trusting you."

Disbelief gave way to tentative hope. "Be serious."

Emma's eyes shone. "I am serious. I've never been more serious in my life."

He didn't want to set himself up for disappointment, but there was nothing in her expression to make him think she wasn't being completely honest right now. No walls. No barriers. Just belief. In him. "But, Em—"

"Just kiss me, Ryan." She brushed her lips against his again. "Something inside of me kept telling me that you wouldn't lie to me like that over and over again. I was afraid to believe, but now I do. It's the truth. You've been innocent all along."

Ryan held her face between his hands. "I can't tell you how happy I am to hear that."

A wave of desire swept through him when he kissed her, more powerful than any he'd felt before—which was saying something. Her hands slid down the front of him

and over his erection. When he pulled back from her, he
saw the raw need in her green eyes.

"I want you," she whispered.

"The feeling is mutual."

He grappled for the handle to the door of his car and
pressed her back against the seat. He felt mindless and
desperate to feel her body clench around his. It swept
away all other thought.

"Just like the teenagers who come to this park," she
managed to say as he worked his jeans off his hips and
tugged her panties down over her legs.

"That's us." Ryan grinned for a moment, but the
expression faded as he quickly slipped on a condom.
Emma's legs fell apart and her mouth pressed hot and
wet against his as he slid into her tight, heated core.

She believed him. He'd felt so alone for so many
months—sometimes he'd wondered if he'd imagined
things and maybe he *wasn't* innocent. But he was and
now she knew it too. Finally.

Now they were making love in a parking lot like a
couple of horny teenagers.

And it felt so damn right.

WHEN EMMA WOKE the next morning she had to remind
herself that the night before wasn't just a dream. She felt a
firm, warm body against hers. A glance over her shoulder
confirmed Ryan sleeping beside her. They'd left the park,
forgotten all about dinner, and come back to her house
where he'd made love to her all night long.

He was innocent. Many people might question her
certainty—and possibly her sanity—considering she
was going solely on his word. She had no confirmation
from anyone else that this Doppelganger potion was a

real thing. She'd heard of similar potions, but not one that totally changed a person's appearance to resemble someone else.

It was far-fetched at best.

But she believed it with all of her heart. She supposed it was an example of faith—she had faith in Ryan, a faith that had never completely been extinguished. It stayed there, flickering deep inside of her until the moment it came time to tap into it. When he told her his story, his theory, everything finally fell into place.

She just wished she'd known he was telling the truth the whole time. It could have saved many months of uncertainty and feelings of betrayal.

She slid her hand over his bare chest, trying to memorize every inch of him. He looked so innocent when he slept.

Her hand drifted lower on his abdomen and slipped past the bedsheets to wrap around his stiffening cock.

Ryan opened one eye. "And I'm awake."

She grinned. "Glad to hear it."

His breathing grew labored. "You know, it's not polite to tease a man first thing in the morning."

"Is that what I'm doing?"

"I'd say so."

"I'm not teasing." She slid down the length of him and peeled back the covers so she could slide her tongue along the length of him. He pressed back into the bed and groaned as she took him fully into her mouth.

"Much better than an alarm clock," he managed to say.

She slid back up his body and kissed him passionately. He slid his hands over her bare back, pressing his erection firmly against her stomach.

"Do you feel it?" she whispered against his lips.

"Oh, I feel it. Definitely."

She smiled. "No. I mean…I thought the Desidero potion's effects would have worn off by now, but they're still working as strong as they ever were."

His fingers dug into her arms as she straddled him. "Seems that way."

She slid her tongue over the curve of his ear. "I want you. Badly."

"The feeling is mutual."

He managed to find a condom and sheath himself before she shifted her hips on top of him, reaching back so she could guide his hard length into her. He groaned deep in his throat. The sensation of having him inside of her was so overwhelming that she needed a moment to catch her breath. Her heart pounded hard in her chest.

"This feeling," she said shakily. "I don't want it to go away. It's so intense, so incredible."

He cupped her breasts, circling his thumbs over her tight, aching nipples, as she began to moved up and down on him. His gaze darkened with desire.

"Emma…" he growled. "You're driving me crazy."

She grinned. "Glad to hear it."

Ryan grabbed her, circling his arms firmly around her and rolled over so he was on top. In this new position, his thrusts became faster, deeper and she felt like she was going to lose her mind to the pleasure he gave her.

She held on to him as he made love to her, arching her back when her orgasm swept through her, followed quickly by his own.

"So…" Ryan said a few minutes later as he traced slow circles on her bare stomach from where he lay next to her in the tangle of sheets. "What do you want to do today? I can think of many things. All which involve us not leaving this bed."

Emma propped herself up on her elbow. "I want to go back to New York and talk to Xavier Franklin."

He eyed her. "That would involve leaving this bed."

"It does. But if he's been buying some of the stolen merchandise, he might know who set you up."

Ryan's easy, relaxed expression tensed. "I was going to take care of that myself."

"Well, guess again. I'm a part of this now, Ryan. And I'm going to do everything I can to clear your name."

He just watched her as if he couldn't believe what she was saying. "You don't know how great it feels to hear you say that."

"Good." She sat up and swung her legs over the side of the bed. "Now immediately after you make love to me again in the shower, we're on our way."

He laughed deep in his throat. "I do like the way you think."

12

By day, the Franklin Mansion looked about the same as it had the other night, only without the masked partiers. Ryan and Emma approached it cautiously. Ryan was determined to get his answers today and be done with it. Then he could take Emma back to Mystic Ridge and continue where they'd left off.

It was the best plan he'd had in recent memory.

Frankly, he was overwhelmed by everything that had happened so quickly. That Emma was ready to believe him had filled him with more hope than he would have thought possible. It was a good thing. This was a very good thing. And he only prayed it would all work out in the end.

When Ryan had been fired, he had to admit that Patrick had been fair with him. Patrick had explained the situation. Explained the evidence. He'd seemed disappointed, but it wasn't the first time an employee had allegedly stolen from the vault, nor was it likely to be the last time. In his view, Ryan had been caught red-handed both on the videotape and by Emma's witness report. Patrick's hands were tied—he had to let Ryan go. He could have filed charges with the police and made it much more difficult for Ryan to move on, but he hadn't. Ryan would always be grateful for that.

But Ryan didn't want his old job back. That wasn't what this was all about. He wanted to clear his name to everyone—to Emma. Then he'd head down to Florida to work with his brother at the garage and start his new life. It seemed like the best idea for him—a chance to work all day surrounded by the cars he loved and reconnect with his big brother who'd turned his life around just as much as Ryan had over the years.

The only problem was, Florida was a hell of a long way from Mystic Ridge.

"Well, here we are," Emma said as they stood at the front door of the mansion. "I can't believe it."

It seemed like a lot more than three days had passed since he'd last been here, ready to confront the old man about his expensive hobby. "So we go in, ask questions as if we're investigating the case officially, and see what we can uncover."

Emma gave him a sexy smile. "Just like the good old days."

They'd made a great team the year they worked together. He couldn't have asked for a better partner. He raised an eyebrow at her. "Have you missed having me around?"

"A little bit."

"Only a little?"

She shrugged. "Wouldn't want it to go to your head."

A grin tugged at his lips. "Are you ever going to admit that the hero in your book is based on me?"

"I don't want that to go to your head, either, so probably not."

His grin widened. "I'll take that as a yes. You know, you should keep writing."

"Oh, yeah?"

"Yeah, you're a natural at it. There's that one scene in the book.... I can't stop thinking about it. It was so sexy. The one with all the candles and rose petals."

Her gaze grew heated. "That is one of my favorites."

"It was pretty...intense." It was the scene where the hero wanted the heroine to know exactly how deep his feelings for her went, beyond sex, beyond desire. Their love was for real. It was written with so much passion, it practically burned his fingers. Of course, at the end of that scene, the hero asked the heroine to marry him and she declined. He went his way and she went hers, leading to a rather unsatisfying ending.

If Ryan was a woman, he'd care more about that sort of thing, of course.

Still, it definitely needed a sequel.

Emma cleared her throat, her gaze sliding over Ryan's body as if she couldn't help the direction of her eyes. "The scene was...fun to write. And I feel like I do have another book in me. Consider me recently inspired. But, uh, can we focus right now, Ryan? I believe there are more important things to deal with. Like, I don't know, clearing your name?"

"Okay, but I'm not finished with this subject. It's important, too."

Emma rolled her eyes. "Consider me forewarned."

"Okay, here it goes." Ryan rang the doorbell and tried his best to look professional.

A minute went by before the door opened. The butler stood there wearing traditional black and white and looking solemn and professional. "Yes?"

"We'd like to see Mr. Franklin," he said.

"I'm sorry, but Mr. Franklin is very busy today. He's not receiving anyone without an appointment."

Emma spoke up first. "Can you tell him that Emma Black from the Paranormal Assessment and Recovery Agency is calling? I was here the other night and he asked me to become his mistress. Please tell him I've given it a great deal of thought."

The butler pursed his lips, gave her a sweeping glance, and his grip tightened on the door. "Please come in."

Ryan repressed a smile. Nice to know that Franklin's staff was well aware of his many passions.

The butler left them standing in the foyer while he went to announce them. The room had a high ceiling with a skylight above them, making the area as bright as outside.

Ryan looked at Emma. "So you've decided to give the idea of having a sugar daddy a chance?"

"Oh, yes," she agreed, straight-faced. "He's so sexy, I just can't help myself."

"Some old guys still have it. In fifty years, I hope I'm half as horny as he is."

Her lips twitched as if she was repressing a smile. "Thank you for your opinion."

It was difficult for him to refrain from touching her. She was so beautiful, so sexy, and he was incredibly tempted to make love to her again right here in the foyer of the Franklin mansion. Although, that probably wouldn't make Franklin all that keen on helping him out. The old man already thought that Ryan was competition for Emma's amorous attentions.

"Should I go hide somewhere?" he asked. "That was a great line to get in here. Don't want my presence to ruin anything."

But it was too late. The next moment, Xavier Franklin marched into the foyer with his attention solely focused on Emma.

"Emma, my dear, it's so wonderful to see you again." He clasped her hands in his and brought them to his lips.

"You too, Xavier."

His gaze moved toward Ryan as if seeing him for the first time. His pleasant expression fell. "Oh, my. This is unexpected."

Ryan moved forward and stretched out his hand. "Great to see you again."

Xavier hesitated only a moment before shaking his hand. "Yes, of course." His gaze flicked to Emma. "Your fiancé is all right with our arrangement?"

She frowned. "Our arrangement?"

"My butler told me that you…" He cocked his head to the side. "I see. You only said that to bring me out to see you, didn't you?"

Emma's gaze didn't waver. "Yes, I did."

Ryan braced himself for the old man's reaction.

"Very clever," Xavier concluded, a smile spreading over his wrinkled face. "Very clever indeed. I won't hold it against you, wicked girl. Obviously you wanted to see me for a very good reason."

"I do. We both do. Can we talk somewhere private?"

"Of course." He led them through the impressive mansion with its chandeliers and inlaid floors, imported wood, gold trim, and high ceilings. It had a rooftop terrace that Ryan spent some time on at the party to escape from the clawing socialite who'd wanted to "get to know him better." As beautiful as she admittedly was, and as much money as she had to back up those looks for the next thirty years at least, he couldn't say he'd been interested at all.

Especially after he'd spotted Emma.

They finally arrived at a very familiar room—the

library. Ryan and Emma exchanged a glance after his gaze moved over the black leather couch where they'd first noticed the potion's effects.

Good times.

"So," Xavier said, after closing the door. "What is it you wished to discuss with me, so much that you'd journey all the way from your quaint little town to mine again? It's not a short trip."

"A little over three hours," Ryan confirmed, crossing his arms over his chest.

"I'm sorry I lied," Emma said. "I didn't think you'd speak to us otherwise."

Xavier pursed his lips and regarded them each in turn. "I am disappointed that you aren't interested in my suggestion from the other night, Emma, but I'm used to dealing with disappointments and moving on from them. Luckily for me, the majority of beautiful women whom I show interest in do not have *fiancés*."

Ryan tried not to laugh out loud at that. Franklin thought the only reason that Emma would reject his proposition was because she was engaged. The laughter died in his throat as Ryan eyed her.

The man *was* a billionaire. That had to be extremely attractive to most women.

But Emma wasn't most women.

He knew this "relationship" he had with Emma probably wouldn't end well. He was going to go to work with his brother fifteen hundred miles away and she'd stay here, where her career with PARA was.

It was best to enjoy everything while it lasted and not think about how it would inevitably come to an end.

Today, he'd force himself to focus on the business at hand.

"We're here on PARA business," Ryan added bluntly,

his good mood falling away like sand through an hourglass. "We know that you have acquired several items that were stolen from our vaults in the last year, as well as other items procured from around the world."

Franklin's face paled. "I don't know what you're talking about."

"Ryan," Emma said sharply. "I don't think that's a very polite way of broaching the subject."

He eyed her with confusion. This was the reason they were there in the first place. Why not broach away?

"Xavier," she soothed, placing her hand on his arm. "Ryan isn't accusing you. He's asking a question, one we, frankly, already know the answer to. You bought a few items for your secret collection, didn't you?"

His chest moved with his rapid breathing. "No."

Ryan rolled his eyes. The old man knew he was in the wrong, but there was no way he was admitting it. This approach wouldn't get them anywhere. Ryan had hoped to use the authority PARA might hold for him to extract the truth.

"It's okay," Emma said. "We're PARA agents, but we're not actually here on official business."

Ryan eyed her curiously, wondering what her game plan was. But because they'd worked so easily together before, he stood back and let her do her thing.

"Then why are you here?" Xavier asked with suspicion.

Emma paced back and forth in a small area, her stiletto heels clicking against the hardwood floor. Today she wore a gauzy blue skirt that swished as she moved and drew Ryan's appreciative gaze to her legs. "Well, the economy isn't great right now, although a man of your wealth and intelligence probably isn't touched much by that unpleasantness. It's amazing what you've done for yourself here."

"Thank you. I've worked very hard."

"And now you deserve to play hard, give parties, spend your money on beautiful women who catch your eye. You also deserve to expand your interests in collecting very unique pieces." She paused. "And we can help you with that collection."

He looked at her skeptically. "You can?"

She glanced at Ryan who watched her with interest. "Ryan and myself are…entrepreneurs, if you will. We are in a position to get our hands on some extremely valuable pieces that, in all confidence, we thought you might be interested in."

Xavier studied her. "Is that so?"

She nodded. "When they came into our possession, the first person I thought of was you. They're glassware, which I know you already collect."

"What kind of glassware?"

"They're five jars that hold the separate pieces of a djinn. It's said that when they're all brought together and a special incantation is read—" She shrugged. "I'm sure you can think of a wish or two you'd like to have granted. Even a man in your enviable position must want something."

"A djinn," he breathed, and his pale eyes lit up.

With every word Emma spoke, Ryan grew more and more impressed with her ability to…well, *lie*. It was a skill he never knew she had.

And it was actually turning him on. Although, with Emma, it didn't take all that much. But he'd never seen this side of her—a side that was willing to do whatever it took to get results. He liked it.

Emma spread her hands. "I wasn't totally certain

you'd be open to a business transaction like this. I saw your public display of glassware, of course, and I'd only heard a few rumors that you were interested in more than that."

Franklin paced to the far side of the room, stood in front of an expansive floor to ceiling bookcase that was packed with leather bound volumes, and then turned to look at them again. "Thank you for coming here, both of you. It is very rare for me to be presented with such a stunning and tempting offer. But I'm going to have to decline."

Emma's eyes widened. "Decline? Why?"

He hesitated for a moment, before a wicked smile lit up his wrinkled face. "Perhaps in the future we can do business together. But right now I think it best to stay with my regular supplier."

Emma and Ryan shared a glance. "So you're currently working with another supplier?" she asked. "I'd be curious to know more about my competition in this area."

"Yes, I'm sure you would be." He looked amused. "I can't help you there, I'm afraid. My dealings with my supplier are confidential. But I'd be happy to show you my valued items, the ones I don't share with just anyone."

Ryan moved to Emma's side, placing his hand on the small of her back as they watched Franklin turn back to the bookcase, pull a book out on the shelf next to him and step back. The bookcase swung around revealing an opening to another room.

Jackpot, Ryan thought.

"Come," Xavier beckoned them and they moved to look into the other room that resembled a wing of a museum. Glass cases, lit up from the inside, showed pieces that Xavier had collected over the years. Pottery, jewel-encrusted boxes no bigger than a deck of cards. Vases, plates, jars, bottles of all shapes, sizes and colors. The old man gazed around at his hidden collection with pride. "These are some of my favorites."

"All glassware," Ryan observed.

"All *erotic* glassware, actually," Xavier corrected with a smile. "My tastes lean toward the more sensual side of history. For example, this necklace—" he placed his hand against a cabinet that held what looked like a small green sphere of jade clasped in a dragon's claw "—when worn by either woman or man will intensify their orgasm by a hundred fold. I made the mistake of wearing this one wild weekend in the sixties. I was in a coma for over a week, but I have to tell you, it was well worth it."

Emma blinked. "That sounds…interesting."

He nodded. "It was."

Ryan repressed a smile. "And how about this one?" He pointed at a small box with roses entwined on the lid. It was also made from glass, dark blue, with a mother of pearl inlay.

"That is less erotic and more filled with melancholy," Xavier said, sobering. "It's where memories of desire can be stored when they become too distracting. Many of my memories of my first wife, Gloria, are kept in there. I only open it when I'm feeling particularly nostalgic."

"She passed away?" Emma asked, gazing through the glass barrier at the box.

"No, she divorced me because I liked to sleep with other women," Xavier said bluntly. "But that didn't mean I didn't love her. One must accept who one is and the people who truly love you in return should be willing to adapt."

Ryan wasn't sure he totally bought that. Hell, he supposed he was a diehard romantic since he believed in monogamy. Outside of a relationship, sleeping around wasn't a problem. But when in a relationship, he was a one-woman man.

Who enjoyed reading erotic romance novels.

Who knew?

"It's an incredible collection," Emma said. "One I think would benefit from a quintet of djinn glassware."

Ryan grinned. "They are definitely not something you're going to see on the home shopping network."

"No, I don't suppose I would." Xavier clasped his hands together. "It does sound incredibly tempting. Perhaps I'll ask my supplier if there's any problem with my dealing with another PARA agent."

Emma's eyebrows went up. "*Another* PARA agent?"

"Yes, and I have a meeting with that agent in—" he glanced at his Rolex "—half an hour. I'm afraid I'm going to have to cut this discussion short so I can deal with that matter. Thank you, though, for coming to see me. It was much appreciated."

Ryan felt stunned, like the wind had been knocked out of him, even though he'd half-expected this outcome all along. Another PARA agent was likely the one who'd set him up that night six months ago. And they were going to be here in only a matter of minutes.

Jackpot, indeed.

13

WHILE IT WAS GREAT TO HEAR their suspicions confirmed, it left Emma with a sick, churning feeling in
her stomach.

"A half hour?" she asked. "And this contact of yours
is another PARA agent? You're absolutely sure about
that?"

"Yes, of course I'm sure." Xavier pursed his lips as he
studied her. "Confidentialities aside, perhaps you might
all wish to work together in the future."

While this ruse was good enough to get Xavier to open
up to them, the last thing Emma needed was for someone
untrustworthy to think she was supplying black market
enchanted objects to the highest bidder alongside Ryan
Shephard, a man who'd already been falsely accused
doing just that. She knew he was innocent, but nobody
else did.

"Xavier." She curled her fingers around his arm and
forced a flirtatious smile to her face. "It's very important
that you say nothing about the fact we were here. While
the saying goes that there is honor among thieves, that's
not really true. Your regular supplier would likely feel

that we were trying to infringe on their territory and they'd try to get us fired."

Ryan nodded. "It happens more often than you might think."

"Then we wouldn't be any help to you in the future, would we?" Emma finished.

The billionaire looked dismayed by this. "No, I suppose you're right."

"I like you, Xavier. And I hope you like me, too."

"Yes." He nodded and his gaze moved to her cleavage. "I like you very much."

Emma had worn this low-cut, thin angora sweater especially for him, despite the heat of the summer day. It was good to see her efforts hadn't gone to waste.

"Then you don't want to get me in trouble, do you?" She tried to make it sound sexy. She braved a look at Ryan—he was trying not to laugh. She glared at him. Really helpful support.

"Of course not." Xavier watched her carefully. "I promise not to say a word."

"Thank you."

"And let me think about the djinn bottles. It does sound incredibly tempting."

"I knew you'd think so. All the possibilities."

He scratched his chin thoughtfully. "I've read that djinn are very difficult to predict. That your wish must be perfectly worded or they'll take liberties to make sure you don't exactly end up with what you wanted."

She had been hoping that he wouldn't know anything at all about djinn so she wouldn't have to elaborate on her story. "I never said it wouldn't be a challenge. But you seem to be the sort of man who can handle something like that."

"I am indeed." He squeezed her hand. "Thank you for stopping by. I'll be in touch."

"I look forward to it."

He looked at Ryan. "Take care."

"Oh, I will," Ryan replied. "And don't worry, we can see ourselves out."

Xavier nodded and gave Emma one last searching look. She wondered if he expected her to throw herself into his arms, overwhelmed by her sudden desire to become one of his mistresses after all.

She hoped she'd reassured him that the only man she wanted to throw herself at was Ryan. After all, it was the truth.

Ryan hooked his arm through hers and directed her out of the library. There was no one in the hallway leading toward the front foyer.

"You're sure you don't want to stay?" Ryan teased under his breath.

"I don't think so."

"He's not your type?"

"I'm afraid not. Even if he was younger, I'm not sure our personalities would mesh."

Ryan glanced over his shoulder back toward the library. "You know, when I shook his hand, I tried to get an empathic read on him. From what I could tell, the guy is genuine. He's not one of the bad guys. He just has a ton of money and he likes to collect pretty things."

"So what you see is what you get?"

"Pretty much." Ryan looked into her eyes. "Not like you."

She raised an eyebrow. "Not like me?"

He stopped walking and gathered her into his arms, pressing her back against the wall by the front door. "I never dreamed you were such an accomplished liar."

He made it sound like a compliment. A big one. "I wouldn't really call what I did lying."

"What would you call it, then?"

She hesitated, distracted by the sensation of having Ryan's warm, muscled frame pressed against hers. The Desidero potion's effects swirled, making it difficult to think. "Uh, creative bargaining."

He grinned. "Right. That sounds good, actually. If you don't continue on as a paranormal investigator or a novelist, you should go into advertising."

"I'll keep that in mind." She scanned the hallway looking for the butler. "So what do we do now?"

His gaze darkened. "Your performance back there makes me think maybe I don't know you as well as I thought I did. You're a woman of mystery."

She laughed. "Yes, so mysterious."

"I was impressed."

"Well, don't be. Even though I was doing it for a good cause, it made me feel bad. A little bit." She frowned. "A *really* little bit. But if it helps us figure out who the real thief is, then it'll be worth it."

"And you're doing it for me."

She looked up at him, surprised to see the depth of emotion in his tone was mirrored in his eyes. This conversation had sounded light and amusing on the surface, but she saw that he was still uncertain about her feelings for him. She'd guarded them to the best of her ability, holding how she felt very close to her chest where it could stay safe.

"You'd be surprised what I'd be willing to do for you, Ryan," she whispered, moving her hands over his shoulders.

He slid his fingers through her long red hair and pulled her closer to him, angling his mouth down to hers so that their lips pressed together. She felt him grow hard against her as the kiss deepened. She let out a little moan against his lips.

"This probably isn't an ideal place to lose our focus and give in to the potion's power right now," she whispered.

"Lose focus." He slid his hand down her side and a shiver of pleasure went through her at his touch. "Another well-worded phrase that means something much less polite. You mean that I should try to keep from getting hard as a rock when in public."

She snorted softly. "Something like that."

"Impossible. Not when I'm around you. Your touch, your kiss, your smell…turns me on no matter where we are. Damn it, Em. I want you so much."

He kissed her again and she returned it as passionately. It didn't matter that they were in the foyer of Xavier Franklin's house. Her desire for Ryan was a driving need that didn't need much to shift it into overdrive.

"Do you want me, too?" he whispered.

She felt breathless. "I get the feeling you know exactly what I want."

"I've kind of tapped into my empathic ability today. I can just feel it."

"The potion—" she interrupted.

"This isn't the potion," he said.

Emma looked up at his face. "What do you mean?"

"The effects dissipate after we give in to our desires."

"But I still feel it."

"One day, that's the most it can last. I read up on it. Consider me an expert on the Desidero potion now. It's been well over a day since we were at the hotel."

"A day?" She drew in a breath. "So it's gone? Completely out of our systems?"

"Yes."

"So this... What I'm still feeling for you—"

His mouth closed on hers and he kissed her, taking her breath away. "It's the way I feel, too. I want you, Emma. The potion was only a push. This is real. And lasting."

Even without the potion to blame, she wanted him as desperately as ever. And now that she concentrated, she knew it was true. It felt different. Before she'd been swept away, wanting him, as if a force outside of herself had pushed them together. This was different. More focused. More acute. And it came completely from inside of her.

She wanted him without any outside influences.

He pulled her around the corner of an open archway, into the large parlor that was the main party room the other night. Emma pressed back against the wall and Ryan's hand slid under her skirt, up her bare thigh, to stroke against the damp fabric between her legs.

When his fingers slipped under the edge of her panties to slide against her sex, she had to cover her mouth with her hand to keep from crying out.

"Even still, this—this...is extremely unprofessional, Ryan," she managed to whisper after a moment.

"That I want to take you right here, right now."

"Uh, yeah."

"But you want me to."

"Yes. But—" Her words cut off when he kissed her and slid his middle finger into her heated core. Her knees nearly gave out right then and there.

"Oh, screw it," she moaned. "Yes...I want you. Here. Now."

Emma fumbled to undo the button at the waist of his

jeans and unzipped him. She reached inside his fly and wrapped her hand around his hard length so she could pull him free.

"You make me crazy," he whispered into her hair. "With or without any damn potion. You're so wet, so hot. I need you."

"I need you, too."

He fumbled to pull a condom from his wallet, quickly ripping it open and sheathing himself. "You're sure?" he asked, very serious. "Right here?"

Instead of answering him with words, she smiled wickedly and turned around to face the wall, reaching back to pull him up against her.

He swore under his breath. "I'll take that as a yes."

She felt him slide her skirt up over her hips and tug her panties down over her hips so she was bared to him. He rubbed the tip of his hard cock against her.

"Please…oh, yes." She moaned as he entered her much slower than she'd expected, stretching her an inch at a time, until he was fully seated within her body.

"You feel so good," he growled.

The sensation of being filled by him swept over her and she gasped, clawing at the wall as he began to pump his hips against hers.

"This is so incredibly unprofessional," she managed to say, looking at him over her shoulder.

"No wonder I was fired." He tried to grin at her but failed. His hands moved to cup her breasts through the thin angora of her sweater, one hand slipping past the low-cut front and under her bra to stroke her pebble-hard nipples.

A wave of pleasure crashed over her, stealing her breath, her thoughts, any inhibitions she still had—not that there were many left. There was something about

Ryan taking her like this that was so exciting. There was no thought, only sensation overwhelming her. She'd never felt like this with anyone before. Only Ryan.

She loved him, beyond sex, beyond anything—and she always had. She wanted him to make love to her every day for the rest of her life.

She wondered what he'd think about an admission like that.

Ryan uttered her name, a raspy cry from deep in his throat as he climaxed. He embraced her from behind, pulling her up against the front of him, his lips tracing the contour of her throat.

"Emma…" His voice was hoarse. "You're so amazing."

She tried to breathe normally, which was a challenge. "Is that a compliment or a general statement?"

"Both."

She turned around in his arms and pressed her mouth softly against his. "Ryan, I want to tell you something."

"What?"

She looked up into his blue eyes. "I'm in—"

The doorbell rang, cutting her off. Startled, they moved further into the party room. The only thing that separated it from the foyer was an open archway. Ryan pulled her further into the corner so they wouldn't be seen.

The footsteps of the butler could be heard, hard soles loud against the marble floor. He opened the door.

"Yes?" he asked, a thin baritone echo of how he'd greeted them only a short time ago.

"I have an appointment to speak with Xavier Franklin." It was a woman's voice.

"Of course. Please come in."

Emma had forgotten how to breathe. She *knew* that

voice. Ryan's grip tightened at her waist and her fingernails dug into his arm. They looked at each other in shock
as recognition dawned on both of them.

"Mr. Franklin is waiting for you in the library."

"I'm a bit earlier than I usually am for our meetings."

"It's fine. He had a meeting with some other people,
but they've left. He made sure to tell me that he'd see you
the moment you arrived."

Emma pressed tighter against the wall, but she could
see a sliver of the hallway. And she saw a sliver of the
blonde woman who accompanied the butler down the
hallway toward the library to see Xavier.

Yes, the woman was very familiar. She should be,
since Emma had known her for more than a year.

It was Charlotte.

Denial clouded her thoughts. "No," she whispered.
"It's impossible. It can't be her."

"Maybe it's a mistake," Ryan replied quietly. "PARA
sent you here to retrieve the potion bottle the other night.
Maybe they sent Charlotte to retrieve something else?
Maybe the real thief is on his way later."

Emma was in shock, but she wasn't that naive. "She
just said that they have regular meetings."

Ryan's jaw was tight. "I am, of course, reaching for
straws right now. I'd rather not think that the woman I
once dated had a large part in trying to ruin my life."

Emma couldn't think straight, but she forced herself to
clear the fog from her mind. They needed answers, that
was why they were here in the first place. And the first
answer just walked through the front door. "We need to
follow them."

She straightened her clothes. Her legs were shaky,
but she summoned the will to take Ryan's hand and pull

him along with her down the hallway, hoping very much that they wouldn't be discovered. As far as Xavier or his butler knew, they'd already left.

Little did he know that they'd stop to have sex by his front door first. If they hadn't, however, they wouldn't have been here to witness Charlotte's arrival.

Ryan pulled Emma to the side, crushing her against his chest as the butler walked by again. Luckily, the man didn't seem to notice them hiding beside a hulking black armoire.

Xavier was still in the now-familiar library. The door was ajar and Emma and Ryan moved close enough to hear the conversation within.

"A pleasure as always, Charlotte." Through the slightly ajar door they could see Xavier approach Charlotte, clasp her hands in his and kiss both of her cheeks. "I'll get right down to business. I'm interested in acquiring a new set of items. I'm hoping that you can help me."

"Of course I can," she replied. "For the right price, of course."

He laughed jovially at this. "A woman who loves money is a woman after my own heart. Yes, I will pay dearly for this if you can get it for me."

"What is it?"

"A set of five glass jars, each containing a piece of a djinn. I have information that leads me to believe that PARA currently has them in their possession."

Emma gasped. That bastard had taken the information from her, then turned right around and given it to someone else. He wanted the jars, but he wanted his regular supplier to get them. Of all the damn nerve.

Not that the jars really existed, but it was the principle of the thing.

Charlotte's eyes widened, more with curiosity than with shock. "May I ask where you got this information?"

Emma held her breath and clutched Ryan's arm. Xavier had just shown that he wasn't very trustworthy. There was a high probability he'd sell her out if it served his purpose.

He shook his head after a moment. "I'm afraid not. My sources are my own."

She exhaled and the knot in her stomach loosened a little. She and Ryan exchanged another glance. Xavier was an opportunistic bastard, but he wasn't totally without a moral code.

Charlotte paced back and forth between the leather couch and bookcase on the left side of the room. "If PARA has these pieces, then I think I might be able to get them for you."

"I'm very glad to hear it."

"It might take a little time though. I'll need to consult with my partner."

Xavier nodded. "Ah, your mysterious partner. When might I meet him or her?"

"Right about the same time you tell me who told you about these jars." She smiled thinly.

Again, Emma worried that the old man might betray her confidence. She was banking on him wanting to keep the lines of communication open, but now she wasn't so sure.

Emma's body still ached pleasantly from being with Ryan only a few minutes ago, but she had to keep her wits about her. She'd trusted Charlotte. They'd been roommates. Emma had always thought of her as family. Someone to be trusted. Someone who knew the value of friendship over cold, hard cash.

The thought that Charlotte had anything to do with

framing Ryan was hard to swallow. But the proof of her guilt stood before them, taking secret meetings and making deals.

Then again, she'd thought she'd seen Ryan take the items from PARA that night. If there was a potion that could make someone look like somebody else, maybe someone was trying to look like Charlotte right now.

But why would they do that? Nobody was here to witness it. Manhattan was a three-hour drive from Mystic Ridge.

"We need to get out of here," Ryan whispered. "Before somebody sees us."

She nodded. "And then what?"

"Then you're going to have a talk with Charlotte later. And I'll need to hunt down Stephen. Since he's sleeping with her, he's either completely ignorant or he's involved. We'll get to the bottom of this."

They quickly left the house, slipping as quietly as possible through the front door, then returned to the car parked in a lot two blocks away.

"I'm sorry, Ryan," Emma said, her heart heavy after what they'd discovered. She'd wanted the truth, but these particular answers were hard to face. She felt like crying, but she held back the tears and tried her best to be strong.

"Sorry?" He looked at her quizzically.

"It's just…Charlotte." She shook her head. "I just can't believe it."

"I think she's kept plenty from you, Em. The other day, she followed me to my motel and threw herself at me."

Emma felt herself grow cold. "She *threw herself* at you?"

"Yes."

"And what happened?" she asked.

"Nothing." Ryan shook his head, a look of amusement creeping back onto his handsome face. "I'm not exactly interested in moving backward. Charlotte's in my past. PARA's in my past, too."

He didn't elaborate, but his words were enough to trigger immediate questions for Emma. "So everything in Mystic Ridge is in your past?"

Ryan frowned. "My brother…he has a garage and he wants me to help him out with it, as equal partners. I'll be working with beautiful cars, something that has always been my first love. Sometimes you just have to take a risk." He grinned and shook his head. "I've realized through this whole experience that that's what life's all about. Risks. And the people who don't take them, don't put themselves out there, are usually not all that happy."

"Sounds like the perfect job for you, actually." Emma nodded. She knew Ryan had a thing for cars. Like, a *big* thing. "Where's your brother's business?"

"Miami."

"Oh." Her stomach sank. "That's a long way from here."

He hesitated. "Yeah, it is. But it's the right move for me, I feel it. Even if I manage to clear my name, I wouldn't go back to PARA."

"Right. It's in your past." Emma swallowed past the rapidly growing lump in her throat. "It's also a long drive back to Mystic Ridge, so we better head out."

They got in the car and Ryan put his hand over Emma's. She turned to look at him.

His gaze was serious and it sank into her. "I really can't thank you enough for believing in me, Em. You don't know what it means."

"It's the least I can do," she said.

His lips twitched into a smile. "And you can't say that we haven't had a lot of fun along the way, no matter what the outcome is."

Fun. It seemed like a very small and unimportant word for what she felt. "Yeah, it's been great."

She didn't know what to make of this conversation. She'd believed what she and Ryan had shared was real. That her feelings for him were real. That he felt something in return for her. But now she was starting to second guess herself.

He was leaving Mystic Ridge. He was moving forward.

Emma wondered what would happen when he was finished here once and for all. Maybe he'd experienced enough of Emma to last him a lifetime.

The feeling wasn't mutual.

But that was just something she'd just have to deal with. After all, life was about taking risks…

14

RYAN DROVE THE ENTIRE DISTANCE back to town, blasting the radio and trying to temporarily take his mind off what they'd found out in the city. If nothing else, he was glad that he knew part of the truth. He was deeply disappointed in Charlotte, but he couldn't say he was totally surprised. The girl *had* come from money. Lots of it. It was only the last few years that she'd had to make ends meet on her own. Charlotte was champagne and caviar, not beer and fast food.

He knew Charlotte hated having no money to buy the shiny things she used to take for granted.

And she *had* been driving that nice little luxury coupe yesterday, hadn't she? He didn't remember her having that when he was still around.

Emma had been quiet on the way home. She'd answered him if he asked her something directly, but otherwise, she seemed lost in her thoughts. He couldn't really blame her.

Emma was so completely different from Charlotte. Emma would never steal. She'd work three jobs before she'd stoop that low, or, more likely, she'd do without, because she wasn't capable of hurting someone only to get what she wanted. No question about it.

Emma.

In most of his relationships, the sex had started out mind-blowing only to become less and less exciting over time. It was the reason he'd resisted taking things with Emma to the next level—because he was afraid that would be it. What they had, their friendship, would be sacrificed.

He'd been wrong. It might have to do with the fact that he really, genuinely liked her. "Like" was such an underrated element of being with somebody. They were friends, he could talk to her, he was interested in what she had to say. She made him laugh.

And the sex… He couldn't get enough of her.

Hell, just thinking about her body pressed against his was enough to make him hard again. He wanted her more every time they'd made love and that hadn't faded a fraction since the potion's effects had dissipated. It was extremely distracting. And extremely exciting.

So he *liked* her. They were friends. But he also craved her touch, her body, her scent, her taste. Everything. She believed in his innocence. She had faith in him. And the thought of leaving her to go to Miami was tying him up in knots.

Yeah. The proof was staring him right in the face.

He was in love with Emma Black.

His grip tightened on the steering wheel and he glanced at her out of the corner of his eye.

Love.

So this is what it feels like, he thought wryly. *Good to know.*

He wasn't sure what he was going to do with this feeling yet. He couldn't remember if he'd actually felt this level of emotion for any one person before. He honestly didn't think so because, truthfully, it was scary as hell.

And it was not on his list of things to do while in Mystic Ridge. No, falling in love with Emma had definitely not been in his plans.

Taking full advantage of the Desidero potion and sleeping with her…sure. Falling in love…nope.

But sometimes things just happened. Them finding each other again after all the misunderstandings—well, maybe that had been fate intervening to let them know they were meant to be together.

But first Ryan had to get to the bottom of the mystery surrounding Charlotte and the stolen supernatural goods. Then he'd have to figure out what came next with Emma. The thought was curiously exciting.

WHEN EMMA CALLED Charlotte later that day, her friend had said she couldn't meet for coffee and dessert right away. She was busy doing errands.

Errands. Some errands.

Charlotte had made no mention that those errands had been in New York City and they'd involved meeting with Xavier Franklin about stolen enchanted merchandise to add to his growing collection.

Just thinking about it fried Emma's insides.

A shiny silver sports car pulled up in front of the café, and parked. Charlotte got out of the driver's side, smiled and waved at her. The vehicle was a far cry from the used car Charlotte had driven until recently. Emma felt like such a fool. Charlotte had told her she'd inherited the money from a distant uncle.

What a load of crap.

"Sorry I'm late." Charlotte gave Emma a quick hug before sitting down across the table from her.

"No problem. I know you've been busy."

"You have no idea."

Yes, actually I think I do, Emma thought bitterly.

She was very careful not to let on what she felt inside. Since Charlotte was an empath she might be able to sense Emma's current animosity.

Emma repressed a wry smile. It was Charlotte herself who'd told Emma how to evade an empath. All she had to do was keep happy thoughts in her head if she was sad. Sad thoughts if she was happy. Etcetera. Only an extremely gifted empath—like Patrick, for example—could tell the difference. Charlotte wasn't that gifted.

She was very good at being bad, though. She wasn't giving away even a hint of intrigue yet.

Emma had a moment of doubt. Could someone else have used the doppelganger potion to impersonate her today?

The shiny car, expensive handbag, and designer shoes weren't conclusive evidence. Not by a long shot.

The waitress came over and took Charlotte's order for a pot of tea and a slice of strawberry cheesecake. When the woman left, Charlotte placed the menu back in the holder on the table.

"So," Charlotte said, looking across the table with concern. "I'm glad you asked me to meet you here, Emma. I wanted to talk to you about something important. Something I'm worried about. You've always looked out for me, so now I want to return the favor."

Emma tensed. Maybe Charlotte was feeling guilty over what she'd done and was ready to confess. Emma was ready to hear it, to know her friend was remorseful. It would make a huge difference to her.

"What is it?" She leaned forward a little to give Charlotte her undivided attention.

"It's Ryan. I know he's still lurking about around town. And I know you're sleeping with him." Charlotte shook her head. "It's just not healthy, Emma. You need to get away from him. He's a bad influence on you."

Emma's stomach sank. "Oh? You think so, do you?"

"I do."

"And may I ask how you know I'm sleeping with him? It isn't exactly public knowledge."

Charlotte raised a thin eyebrow. "If I had any doubts, you've just confirmed it for me."

Well, hell.

"What can I say?" Emma held up her hands, deciding to play along. "I think it was kind of inevitable that I'd succumb to his charms one day."

Charlotte's tea arrived and she dunked the tea bag in, pushing it down into the hot water with the back of her spoon. "Maybe. But you need to stay away from him. I understand how you feel. I was involved with him, too. But he's a con artist. He'll make you believe he's in love with you and then he'll use you and walk away without a backward glance."

Emma's blood pressure rose with every word that came out of Charlotte's mouth. She desperately wanted to casually mention that she knew Charlotte had thrown herself at Ryan at his motel yesterday, and that he'd turned her down.

Happy thoughts only.

Bottom line, she now trusted Ryan and she didn't trust Charlotte, come what may. This shift in her perception meant that the man was now fully capable of breaking her heart into a million pieces if he chose to. It was dangerous to give all your trust to one person, but sometimes it wasn't an option. It simply was.

"I guess I just wish I had somebody like Stephen,"

Emma forced the words out. "He's so reliable, so trust-worthy."

"You make him sound like a family doctor." Charlotte grinned. "That's not too sexy."

Emma took a slow sip of her cappuccino. "Depends on the doctor. But what I meant was that you really lucked out when you two hooked up."

Charlotte leaned back in her seat as she added a packet of sugar substitute to her tea. "It's true. Stephen and I are perfect for each other. We want the same things out of life—a great future, adventure, love. The works."

Emma fixed an even smile on her face. "Well, Char-lotte, I truly hope you get everything you deserve."

She really, really meant it.

RYAN WAITED AT A British-style pub called O'Grady's where he knew Stephen went every night at eight o'clock for a beer and a game of darts. It was a ritual they used to share.

If Charlotte was in on this, Stephen likely was, too. And Ryan wanted to know, for sure, if Stephen was the "partner" Franklin had referred to at his mansion earlier.

If so, then Ryan's ex-girlfriend and his best friend had conspired to destroy his life. That didn't sit well with him. At all.

Right on time, Stephen walked in. Ryan sat on a stool at the bar and tried to pretend he wasn't laying in wait, like a hungry lion watching a back-stabbing gazelle ap-proach a slow-moving river to quench its thirst.

"Holy shit," he heard from behind him. "Ryan Shep-hard?"

Ryan forced surprise to show on his face as he turned

around. "Stephen Robbins. What the hell are you doing here?"

"What am *I* doing here? I should ask you the same question." Stephen wore a short-sleeve button-down shirt and black pants. Ryan couldn't help but note the expensive Italian loafers. And that wasn't all that had changed. Stephen's light brown hair wasn't as messy as it used to be. Instead, it was styled, which made Ryan think his old friend had been going to a salon and paying big bucks to try to look like something out of GQ. And he wore a gold Rolex on his left wrist, a lot like the one Xavier Franklin had sported. It wasn't exactly something your average paranormal investigator could afford.

Ryan wasn't an official investigator anymore, but even he could spot the clues when they were so blatantly obvious.

"Yeah," Ryan grinned. "I'm back."

Stephen glanced over his shoulder, as if scanning the bar to see if anyone would witness him speaking with someone who was *persona non grata* in the general area. Then he slid onto the stool directly next to Ryan. "It's seriously great to see you. I've missed you, man."

"Thanks." Ryan tried to loosen his grip on the mug of draft in front of him. Stephen was acting too friendly. This would be much easier if he was a complete dick.

"You doing okay?" Stephen asked after he flagged down the bartender and ordered a mug of the same beer Ryan was drinking.

"Never better."

Stephen frowned. "I'm surprised you're here. Any reason? Or are you just looking for trouble?"

"I'm looking for trouble all right. I'm here because of Emma."

"Oh, yeah?" Stephen's brows went up. "What about her?"

"What do you think?"

Stephen studied him for a moment before his smile returned. "She is pretty damn hot."

"She is."

He snorted. "I will admit to having a few fantasies involving those sexy high heels she wears."

Ryan tried to ignore the stab of jealousy that statement brought forth. They were just two guys talking at a bar. Casual. He had to draw out the truth any way he could. Punching Stephen in the face might not help matters.

"I'm not sure Charlotte would approve of those fantasies," Ryan said pointedly.

Stephen looked at him guardedly. "So I'm guessing that you know about me and Charlotte."

"That would be a good guess."

He shrugged. "Sorry. You were out of the picture and she was available."

Ryan watched the bartender move to the end of the counter and wipe the top off with a wet cloth. This was his chance. He'd decided that his best plan of attack was to try to drive a wedge between Stephen and Charlotte, which might help loosen Stephen's tongue. He didn't have to reach too far to figure out a way to do just that.

"Charlotte hit on me yesterday," he said.

"What?" Stephen growled.

"She followed me to my motel yesterday and kissed me. In fact, she wanted to do more than that, but I told her to get lost."

Stephen stared at him incredulously. "Charlotte kissed you. Yesterday."

Ryan waved his hand flippantly. "Don't worry, I'm not interested in her anymore."

"I think you should leave now," Stephen said in a menacing tone. "I'd forgotten that you're not wanted around here anymore. We don't like thieves and liars."

Ryan studied his face. This man had been his friend. And there was a chance that Stephen knew nothing about Charlotte's dealings with Franklin. If so, Stephen needed to separate himself from the situation as fast as he could.

"Charlotte..." he said. "She's no good. And she's going to drag you down if you let her."

"Listen carefully to me, Shephard," Stephen said between clenched teeth, "If you go near Charlotte again, you'll be sorry. Stick with your little smut writer."

Ryan's shoulders stiffened. "Excuse me?"

Stephen glared at him. "Charlotte told me that Emma wrote a dirty book and is trying to keep it a secret from everyone." He smirked. "I guess that means she's a hellcat in the sack, right? Who knew?"

Ryan curled his hand into a fist at his side and counted to ten in his head. He wasn't going to get any answers from Stephen tonight. His former friend had always been a hothead, quick to anger. "I think it was a mistake to come here."

"You're right. It was."

Ryan forced a smile, but his jaw was clenched. "See you around, Stephen."

Stephen's gaze was narrowed as Ryan slipped off his stool and started toward the door. "Just stay the hell away from Charlotte."

"Don't worry," Ryan replied under his breath as he pushed through the exit door. "She's all yours."

He wanted nothing to do with his lying, cheating ex. Besides, he much preferred his sexy hellcat.

15

EMMA STAYED OUT WITH Charlotte for two hours, trying to get to the truth. But the truth didn't show up. And Emma had to be careful. She couldn't show her hand completely. It would have been great if she could have just come right out and asked, "Hey Charlotte, saw you at Xavier Franklin's mansion today. Did you screw Ryan over, steal from the vault and pin it on him to make some extra cash, you selfish bitch?"

But she couldn't. And it probably wouldn't have gotten her the proof she needed to clear Ryan's name in any case.

She wondered what would happen when and if they were able to prove his innocence. It didn't take very long before she knew. He already told her his plans. He was going to move to Florida and work with his brother. He hadn't considered any other alternatives.

It was a windy drive back to her house. Emma ran a hand through her hair, pulling out tangles as she went and grabbed her cell phone to check the call display. There were no messages from Ryan. They'd parted ways when she went to meet Charlotte. He was going to go see

Stephen. Maybe they'd decided to hang out together and catch up.

She considered dialing his number or texting him, but decided that it could wait until tomorrow. It was getting late. She parked the car in her garage, pulled the door down behind her, and walked up to her front door, key in hand.

But then she stilled.

Something felt off.

Emma turned around where she stood but she wasn't sure what it was. A feeling.

Instead of putting her key into the lock, she tried the doorknob. It turned smoothly in her hand.

The door was unlocked.

"Okay," she whispered. "That's not good."

She slid her hand into her purse and pulled out her gun. A woman living alone really couldn't be too careful these days, even in a low-crime town like Mystic Ridge.

The weapon had been a birthday present from her mother four months ago.

Despite an initial reluctance to carry a gun, Emma liked having it on her for peace of mind. But she'd never found a reason to use it, other than target practice at the firing range she occasionally visited. PARA didn't require its agents to carry weapons—the job was not typically a high-risk one, aside from errant potions, curses, or ghosts—and bullets weren't much use on them anyway.

She nudged the door open with her shoulder, planning to take a quick peek inside before falling back and calling the cops. The first thing she saw was a candle on the small table next to the stairway. It was lit.

"A candle," she said under her breath. "I've got a thief who likes ambient lighting."

There was a candle on each of the wooden steps leading to the second floor. She raised an eyebrow.

"A thief who doesn't mind causing a fire hazard."

She now had a funny feeling she knew who her "thief" was. Keeping the door open with her knee, she glanced over her shoulder and spotted a familiar car parked across the street.

"Right." She closed the door so it didn't make much more than a soft click. "After all, breaking and entering is *such* a good way to win friends and influence people, Ryan."

Emma walked up the stairs slowly, gun still in hand but pointed at the floor. She could be wrong, but she really didn't think so.

She nudged open her bedroom door and her breath caught.

It was the scene from her novel *Inevitable,* the one right near the end. The room was filled with light from a hundred lit candles. Her bed, with its white duvet, was scattered with red rose petals. It was beautiful and it took her breath away.

"Well?" Ryan asked. She glanced over her shoulder to see him standing at the top of the stairs with two glasses of wine in hand.

"Am I dreaming?" she asked.

"No."

"So what you're telling me is you broke into my house when I wasn't here and lit a million candles in my bedroom."

His gaze moved to the gun she held. "Hmm. So you're saying this wasn't one of my more brilliant ideas?"

She tried very hard not to smile. "I could have shot you."

"When did you become Annie Oakley, anyway?"

"Recently. A woman has to protect herself from... undesirables."

"I'm feeling a bit threatened now that I'm facing a strong-willed, armed and dangerous woman," Ryan said, and he grinned. "It's kind of kinky."

A hint of laughter escaped her.

He placed the wineglasses down on her dresser. "I'm sorry. Maybe this was a stupid idea."

Her gaze swept the room again. "This is from my book, isn't it?"

"Yeah." He grimaced, and waved a hand at the fantasy he'd created for her. "Ta da."

After putting the gun back into her purse, then pushing the bag in the corner, she took hold of his shirt and drew him closer to her. "As surprises go, this is actually really sweet."

"Perhaps I'll let you know about any future surprises ahead of time. Of course, then they wouldn't exactly be surprises anymore, would they?"

"Or maybe I'll just give you a key to my house." She made the offer without thinking and then bit her bottom lip. "I mean, if you want one."

He raised an eyebrow. "A key to Emma Black's private home. This is quite an honor. Then I wouldn't have to pick the lock."

"That was the general idea." She glanced at the wine. "I think I need that."

Ryan gave her one of the glasses. "Rough night?"

Her momentarily pleasant mood soured. "I can't believe Charlotte would do something like this."

"I can't believe it either."

She looked at him sharply. "You dated her."

He shrugged. "She was hot."

She frowned for a moment, and then sighed. "You know, I can't really argue with that."

Ryan slid his hand down her arm. "You're hotter."

She couldn't help smiling, and she felt a flutter of emotion in her chest. "Yeah, right."

"You don't have to believe me. The fact that I know I'm telling the truth is enough for me." He slid his fingers into her hair. "Did you find anything out?"

"Nothing. Not one damn thing that would substantiate her being the thief who supplied Xavier Franklin and who knows how many other collectors with stolen merchandise."

"I'm sorry."

"Don't be sorry." Emma looked up at him. "You're the one who should be frustrated. We're trying to clear your name and we keep coming up against brick walls."

"Speaking of brick walls, I spoke with Stephen. I didn't get anything from him, empathic or otherwise. I can't tell if he's got anything to do with Charlotte's schemes or not. I do know he hates me. When I told him about Charlotte coming on to me, he didn't take it very well."

Emma frowned. "Did you get into a fight?"

"Not tonight. But it's only a matter of time if I stay around town much longer."

She shook her head. "Anything I can do to help?"

He raised an eyebrow. "A kiss might help."

"Way to keep your mind on the problem at hand."

He grinned. "Is that a no?"

She glared at him, but then couldn't help but smile. She tugged on his shoulders for him to lean over a little and she brushed her lips against his. "How's that?"

His gaze heated. "A nice start."

When she'd returned to her house, she hadn't felt anything but disappointment over Charlotte and a gnawing feeling in her stomach that things weren't going to turn out well. Now, all she felt was an aching need for this man who stood in front of her. She was afraid her feelings for him would only lead her to heartbreak, but she tried not to worry about that now.

The lust potion's effects were gone, which meant what she felt for Ryan was the real deal. There was no magic at work here other than honest-to-goodness desire.

"I'll tell you the truth," she whispered, pulling his face down to hers.

"What's that?"

"You've been trying to get me to admit that my hero in the book is inspired by you?"

"And?"

"He was. And now I have this burning need to write another one. I thought I'd gotten it out of my system, but…so many fantasies are running through my mind." She shook her head. "It's very distracting."

A smile stretched his lips, but he didn't say anything.

"I've wanted you for a long time, Ryan. It's crazy, I know. When you were with Charlotte, I was really jealous. I crumpled those feelings up in a ball and tried to throw them away so it wouldn't affect me. And then, when I saw you—when I *thought* I saw you steal that night—it helped me push them back even faster. When I was writing the book though, everything just sort of poured out. I didn't even do it consciously. I didn't realize at the time that Bryan was based on you, although now it's totally obvious to me. Everything I felt was thrown into that book. Maybe that's why I don't like very many

Michelle Rowen 185

people to know I wrote it, because it shows too much of what's going on inside me."

"All I can say is that it's an honor you felt that way about me." He frowned. "Well, except for the part when you hated my guts."

"I never hated your guts."

"Sure you did."

"I wanted to. But I didn't. And when I saw you at the masquerade party...it brought everything back. Everything I'd felt, everything I'd fantasized about." She glanced at the bed strewn with rose petals. "And now this."

"Overkill?" He raised an eyebrow.

She grinned. "Nope. It's perfect, actually."

Ryan slid his fingers into her hair. "You do crazy things to me, Em."

She almost laughed. "That's one way to put it."

He snorted softly, but his gaze deepened. "I mean you do crazy things to me here." He took her hand in his and pressed it against his chest, over his heart.

Her own heart twisted and she felt that little part of her that was still hanging on, dangling on the side of the cliff, let go completely and fall...down...down...

Ryan kissed her and there were no more troubled thoughts, no worries, no stress about the future. There was only here and now. With Ryan. The man of her fantasies. The man of her reality.

Emma tugged at his shirt and he broke off the kiss long enough for her to pull it off over his head. Then she slid her hands down the hard planes of his chest and down his rippled abdomen.

"I want you, Ryan." Her voice was raspy.

Any previous humor departed and she could see the

need she felt for him reflected in his expression. "I want you, too."

She smelled the soft, sweet scent of the rose petals as he pressed her back against the bed. His hands fumbled as he helped her pull off her sweater, unhooked her bra, and bared her from the waist up. His eyes raked over her and his gaze darkened.

"You're so beautiful," he whispered hoarsely.

"You're not so bad, yourself." Her hands were at the waist of his jeans and she quickly undid the button and slid the zipper down, then pushed the pants down over his hips so she could wrap her hand around him. She kissed his chest, sliding her lips and tongue down lower. She didn't do more than slide her tongue over the tip of his cock before he pulled back. She looked up at him with surprise.

"What is it?"

"There's time for that later," he said. "But right now it's my turn."

He nudged her back onto the bed and undid her skirt, pulling it off, leaving her there wearing only her panties. He stepped out of his jeans and pushed off his shoes and socks.

"Damn it, you make me so hard, Em," he said.

She hooked her fingers into the sides of her panties and pulled them off, then leaned back against the silky bed spread and parted her legs to bare herself to him. "Then what are you waiting for?"

He grinned, his chest moving with quickening breath. "You are a wicked woman."

She grinned back at him. "You have no idea."

"I think I do have an idea now. Cool on the surface, but hot as lava underneath."

She pulled him down on top of her, hooking her hands

behind his neck and kissing him, spreading her legs wider so she could feel his hard cock brush against the slickness of her sex. "Enough talk, Ryan. I need you inside of me. Now."

His smile grew slightly more wicked. "But then this would be over way too soon."

She groaned, and dug her fingers into his buttocks. *"Please."*

"You can be polite all you like," he whispered in her ear. "But you're going to have to be patient."

He pulled her hands away from him and stretched them up over her head, pressing them against the pillow. His lips brushed along her cheek to her lips, then down over her chin and throat. He stopped to suckle each nipple, drawing each hard peak into his hot, wet mouth, his tongue circling the tip until Emma writhed beneath him and moaned his name incoherently.

"You like that?" he asked.

She was growing short on patience already. "Ryan... please..."

"I'll take that as a yes."

She felt the scratch of his stubble over her sensitive stomach, his tongue tracing the contour of her navel, her hip bone, her inner thighs. Her body quaked and shivered with each press of his lips and tongue against her sensitive flesh.

When she felt the hot slide of his tongue against her sex, circling her clit, she stopped thinking entirely. She arched off the bed as he made love to her with his mouth. She reached down and grabbed the back of his head. He looked up at her, his gaze dark and filled with desire.

He continued to stroke her with his tongue until she cried out, her body wracked with the most exquisite pleasure she'd ever felt. It was such intense pleasure it was akin to pain, every cell in her body seeming to explode into a shimmer of passion.

The world blurred before her eyes and then Ryan was at her mouth again kissing her, his tongue tangling with hers. She could taste herself on his lips and tongue. She couldn't speak, only feel.

He managed to sheath himself with a condom he'd grabbed from his jeans pocket. When she felt him against her, his hands raising her hips off the bed so he could fill her in one deep thrust, her vision went bright at the edges as another orgasm swept over her, leaving her entire body shaking.

The Desidero potion had made it impossible not to want Ryan. But now, even though its effects had abated, she only wanted him more. He was everything to her. And as he moved inside her, whispering her name over and over in her ear, his lips brushing against her shoulder, her jaw, her lips, she was sure that she told him what she truly felt. She could hear it, but she wasn't certain whose lips spoke the words or if it was some sort of psychic connection only forged in the deepest heat of passion.

"I love you."

If it was she who spoke the words, it didn't lead to any immediate worry that her feelings wouldn't be reciprocated. It simply was. She loved him. And that love didn't come with any strings. Not right now.

His thrusts became faster and deeper and she clung tightly on to him until, with one last press of his hips against hers, he swore gutturally as he came and then groaned her name, a shuddery sound against her lips when he kissed her again.

Ryan's body weight pressed her down against the mattress as they lay there still and silent. After a moment, he pushed up onto his forearms and looked down at her, then brushed the hair back from her forehead.

She stared up into his eyes, trying to memorize every angle of his face, every feature, every line.

"That…" she said after she regained the ability to speak, "…should be illegal."

A smile broke through his very serious expression. "I have to agree. Em, you're so…"

Emma managed a sigh. "So amazing? Sexy? Incredibly addictive?"

"I thought you were a clairvoyant, not a mind reader." He kissed her. "All of that and so much more."

"The feeling's mutual, Shephard."

He brushed his lips against her collar bone. "I figured you wouldn't be able to resist the temptation of rose petals and flickering romance. I have to admit, it took forever to light them all."

She went silent for a moment, lost in her thoughts.

He frowned down at her. "Something wrong?"

"No, it's just…something you said."

"I know, I promise no more breaking and entering. But it just seemed like such a good idea at the time. I will remember to use my brain next time and not just my imagination."

"It's not that." A thousand thoughts were running through her head all at once. "I think I know what we need to do," she said, excitement coloring her voice.

Ryan shifted position so he lay on his side next to her, his hand splayed across her stomach helping to warm her. "What?"

"Charlotte wouldn't reveal anything to me tonight, nothing that could determine who she was working with."

His brows drew together. "I know. It's going to be tricky to find the truth."

Emma smiled wickedly. "But that's just it. We *have* to be tricky."

He just looked at her, confused. "Meaning what?"

"Meaning what you just said a minute ago…about figuring out what I wouldn't be able to resist, what would be the best way to lure me into your tempting little trap."

He groaned. "Not sure I'd describe it as a trap—"

She pouted. "Are you going to let me finish or what?"

"Sorry, sorry. Please, Ms. Black, tell me what you plan to do to help me clear my good name and find the real thief once and for all."

She pushed him back onto the bed and climbed on top of him so she could look down at his face. Bracing her palms against his firm chest, she said, "We're going to set a trap. And then we're going to see who's greedy enough to fall into it."

"A trap."

"Yes."

"Set with what?"

"I have an idea of something our prey should have a very difficult time resisting."

"Sounds risky."

She smiled. "I believe it was you who said that life is all about taking risks."

Ryan slid his hands up her body and cupped her breasts. "You know, you are as devious as you are beautiful."

Emma leaned over and kissed him. "I will take that as a very big compliment coming from you."

He grinned. "As you should."

16

CHARLOTTE PICKED UP after the second ring. "Emma?" She sounded surprised. "What's up?"

"Sorry to call you so late," Emma replied, trying to inject a great deal of raw emotion into her voice. Ryan sat next to her on her sofa, his arm curled around her back.

"What's wrong?"

Emma inhaled shakily. "It's… Oh, God, Charlotte. You were right about Ryan."

"Of course I was right, Emma. He's bad news."

"I'm just such a fool. He came back to town and he tried to convince me that he wasn't the person who robbed the PARA vaults, that somebody had set him up. But it wasn't true. I'm almost completely positive it was him."

"*Almost* positive?" Charlotte sounded surprised. "But you saw him yourself."

"I did, but…he kept talking the other night and I started to doubt myself. I mean, I guess I could have been wrong. It could have been a trick of the light, or the darkness, or… I don't know. But maybe it wasn't him—at least, that's how I was feeling. But now, I'm not so sure he's not just setting me up."

Charlotte sighed. "Is Ryan in town very long? Do you know?"

"I don't know. But…but that's not really the reason I called. I need your advice."

There was a pause. "With what?"

"I have some pieces in my possession right now. I brought them home to catalogue them over the weekend and I'd planned to take them back to PARA tomorrow so they can go into the vault. But I'm not sure if they're safe in my house. I made the mistake of mentioning them to Ryan when he stopped by earlier and his eyes seemed to light up. I'm afraid he might come back tonight and try to steal them."

"Pieces? What kind of pieces?"

"Something that we just got in last week. Glass jars— five of them. Apparently they have some sort of spirit trapped inside."

"Spirit—" Charlotte's voice turned sharply curious, right on schedule. "What kind of spirit?"

"The paperwork says that they date back to the Persian Empire and that they have a djinn connection. They were found in a small antiques shop in England and have already caused some trouble there. Instead of sending an agent to collect them, they were couriered to PARA."

"You have djinn jars in your house right now," Charlotte said incredulously. "You're kidding me."

"I'm not kidding. But I'm not totally convinced they're legit. I sense some otherworldliness coming from them, but if there's a djinn inside, he's hiding really well."

"They might be fakes."

"That's very possible."

"But if they're not…" Charlotte went silent for a

moment. "They'd be worth a lot of money to certain people. People like *Ryan*."

"That's exactly what I was thinking. Do you think they're safe here? Or should I return them to PARA right now? Better safe than sorry, and all that."

"Even if Ryan's tempted, he'd have to be really ballsy to try to steal them right out of your house. I don't think even he'd go that far."

Emma's grip on the phone tightened, as did her other hand, which rested on Ryan's leg as if using him as her anchor. "But if he did, that would tell me the truth, once and for all. I'd know for sure that he's a lying, thieving scumbag that I don't want anything to do with." She glanced at him apologetically. He brought her hand to his lips and kissed it.

No apology necessary.

"Yeah, definitely," Charlotte said. "Still, I don't think he will risk it. I think the jars are safe right where you have them."

"The cabinet right next to my TV has a lock," Emma supplied. She'd gone over the story with Ryan at least ten times to make sure it sounded believable. "I hope they'll be okay in there till tomorrow."

"I think they'll be fine. So you're all right, Emma? Or do you need me to come over for some moral support?"

"No, I'm fine. I'm probably going out in a minute, anyway. The fresh air'll help clear my head a bit. Besides, I've got to get some groceries. The weekend's really gotten away from me."

"Time flies when you're fulfilling your fantasies with bad boys."

Emma let out a shaky laugh. "Some moral support."

"I aim to please." There was a smile in Charlotte's voice now. "I'll see you tomorrow, Emma."

Once she heard Charlotte disconnect, Emma hung up the phone and turned to Ryan.

"Did she sound like she suspected anything?" he asked.

"I don't think so."

He nodded. "Good. So now we wait and see if anyone shows up." He stood up and went around the room flicking off the lights.

Xavier Franklin himself had made a special request for the jars—and the man had money to burn. If Charlotte had anything to do with the initial crime and money was her motivation, she'd find a temptation like this completely irresistible.

They were close. So close.

After an hour went by with nothing, Ryan swore under his breath.

"What?" Emma asked.

"My car. I just remembered it's parked across the street."

She grinned at the memory. "Luckily it was, or I might have shot you earlier."

He looked worried. "Yeah, but if anyone spots it, they'll know I'm here. '68 Mustangs aren't parked on every corner."

Emma's grin faded. "That might be a problem."

"I'll go move it."

She nodded. "Hurry."

"I will."

Ryan kissed her quickly, then got up from the sofa and went to the front door, opening it and closing it behind him with a soft click. Emma glanced over at the locked cabinet where she'd told Charlotte she'd hidden the jars.

Inside were some DVDs and a stack of manuals for the washing machine and microwave oven. No jars.

But the glassware didn't really have to exist for it to bring a thief out of hiding. Especially when Emma said she'd be out of the house doing some late night grocery shopping.

Reveal the thief, clear Ryan's name, and then...well, then she didn't know what would happen next.

One thing at a time.

RYAN JOGGED ACROSS the street to where his car was parked. His mind still swam from the time he'd spent with Emma tonight. Every moment spent with her was better than the last. She was amazing. He couldn't just pick up and leave town and risk never seeing her again.

No, he couldn't do that. He actually had no idea what he was going to do next.

He heard footsteps on the pavement behind him. For a moment he thought that Emma had followed him outside, but he didn't recognize the sound of her high heels. He turned to take a look at the person following him and froze in place.

It was...*him*.

Or, rather, it looked exactly like him. Even the clothes—jeans and a black T-shirt.

"Okay," he said slowly. "At least this clears up one of the mysteries."

"You shouldn't have come back," his twin said. Even the voice sounded identical to Ryan's.

"Infringing on your territory, am I?" Ryan tried his best to keep his voice calm and collected.

"You being here just makes things more difficult for me." The man cocked his head to the side. "Except for occasions like this when you're making things much easier."

His gaze swept Ryan's body. "I was going to switch our clothes, but I think I'm close enough."

"Yeah, you win the stuffed panda. Congrats." Ryan glared at him. "Doppelganger potion?"

"It's rare stuff."

"It must be very convenient, working for an agency that happens to have a department for rare potions, isn't it?"

His twin grinned. "I'm afraid we're going to have to bring this fascinating conversation to an end."

"You're not getting past me," Ryan said, clenching his hands into fists at his sides. "There's no way."

"Where there a will there's a way, Ryan. And I suggest you stay out of my very willful way if you know what's good for you."

Ryan took a step forward, ready to wrestle the man down to the ground when he sensed someone behind him. He wasn't able to turn in time before he felt a painful crack against the back of his skull and everything went black.

"How LONG DOES IT TAKE to park a car?" Emma mumbled to herself as she got up from the sofa. Just as she reached the front door, it opened in front of her.

Ryan's eyes fixed on her and a smile stretched across his handsome face. "I'm back."

She sighed and it came out shaky. "Any problems?"

"No, none. Any with you?"

"Other than the fact that somebody I considered family has turned out to be a selfish, lying bitch? No, that about covers it."

Ryan's jaw tightened almost imperceptibly. "She's definitely a handful, that's for sure."

"Yeah." It was rough whenever she let herself think

about it too long. "It sucks putting your trust in somebody and having them lie to your face."

"I'm sorry you've had to go through all of this pain, Emma."

"Me, too." She glanced out the small window, then closed the drapes. "So I guess we just keep waiting."

"All vigilant."

"That's us."

"Where do you want to wait?"

"Back in the living room's fine." She led the way and sat down heavily on the sofa. Ryan sat down next to her. He seemed tense. She wasn't surprised.

"So what do you think's going to happen?" she asked.

He leaned back, pressing his tall frame into the soft material. "The bad guys get caught and the good guys ride off into the sunset. Right?"

She tensed. "This isn't a movie."

"Well, obviously we're doing this to clear my name."

"We are."

"And you believe that I'm totally innocent, right?"

"With all my heart."

Ryan turned to her and swept the hair back from her face, tracing a line down the side of her throat. "You're a very beautiful woman, Emma."

What was he doing? This wasn't the time to get amorous, not when they were waiting for a break and enter to happen. "Well, thank you. And you know, I don't really mind it as much as I said I do."

"Mind what?"

"The name you use for me."

Ryan smiled. "The one you don't like me to call you, right? I have many special names for you." His hand drifted down over her collarbone to her left breast. "Perhaps we should explore each of them."

She glanced in the direction of the front door. "As delightful as that sounds, I think we have a couple of other things to take care of first. If somebody shows up tonight, whether it's Charlotte or somebody else, we can't be in bed."

He leaned closer to whisper in her ear and his fingers drew circles around her nipple through the thin material of her shirt. "But I really want you, Emma. I want to make every fantasy in your naughty little book come true."

He wasn't being half as serious tonight as she would have expected, considering what was on the line for him. "I'm going to have to be strict with you."

"Oh, yes, please. I think I'd like that."

As pleasant as his hands felt on her, reminding her of what had happened between them earlier upstairs, something felt off.

"Maybe later," she said.

"Promises, promises." His hand was now on her thigh, moving higher. Then he kissed her, his tongue searching for hers.

"Ryan—" She leaned back a bit, pressing her palms against his chest. "You're acting really strange right now."

"Sorry. We're protecting something very valuable. I keep forgetting."

She eyed him. "Yeah, if air is valuable, that's what we're protecting."

He pulled away from her suddenly. "Oh, yeah," he said slowly. "Right. It's just a ruse to lure the thief here. Nothing to steal at all, is there?"

"Just try to behave yourself."

He smiled thinly. "I'll do my best."

WHEN RYAN WOKE, he wasn't sure how long he'd been unconscious but his head felt like it had been trampled by a herd of elephants and then used for batting practice by the New York Mets.

He was in an enclosed dark space. He pressed his hands above his head and then swore under his breath.

His twin and the man's associate had locked him in the trunk of his car. Bastards. The air was musty, but breathable. Car trunks were not airtight. Or impossible to escape from.

His doppelganger had seen one too many gangster movies.

It didn't take long before he found the latches and pushed down the seats so he could slip out of the car.

He scanned the area. Nobody was around. He grabbed his cell phone, which sat on the front seat. A quick check at the time told him it had only been ten minutes since he'd come outside in the first place. Not bad. But not good. That meant his doppelganger was...

His body tensed. He didn't want to think about it. He just needed to *do* something about it.

Grabbing the phone, he dialed a number that he knew from memory. Emma's house. He had to warn her.

The phone kept ringing and no one picked up. Finally the call went to voicemail. He swore under his breath, pressed the disconnect button, and tried another number.

The recipient picked up on the third ring.

"McKay."

"Patrick..." Ryan's voice came out hoarse and his head felt like it was on fire. "This is Ryan. Ryan Shephard."

"Ryan Shephard? Are you serious?"

"Yes, I know you think I'm the son of a bitch who stole from you, but don't hang up."

"Give me one good reason why I shouldn't."

"I'll give you two reasons."

And then he launched into the quickest, most ridiculous story he'd ever told anyone in his entire life.

It was, of course, all true. But whether Patrick would believe him was another matter altogether.

17

WITH EVERY MINUTE THAT PASSED, Emma was less and less certain that they'd been right. Maybe it was true. Maybe Charlotte didn't have anything to do with the thefts. The woman's conversation with Xavier today was extremely damning, but maybe there was another explanation.

"I'm not sure what to do," she said out loud a few minutes later.

"About what?" Ryan asked.

"About everything."

"Are you talking about the thief or about us?"

She looked at him. "I was talking about the thief, but now that you mention it…"

"What?"

It wasn't something she'd meant to discuss tonight, but now that the opportunity presented itself… "*Is* there an us?"

He raised a dark eyebrow. "I think that's a question you need to answer for yourself."

She chewed her bottom lip. "Yeah, but it's a scary one."

"Why's it scary?"

"Because it just is."

"That's not a very good answer. I thought you were a wordsmith. You and your little book." He settled his hand on her left thigh, just under the edge of her skirt.

"Yeah, me and my book." She sighed. "I started writing down my fantasies because I needed something I wasn't getting from my regular life. I was able to disappear into those fantasies. I mean, I guess you know that. You recreated one of them earlier upstairs."

"I'd like to bring all your fantasies to life, Emma."

"There's time for that." Then she paused. "Unless there isn't time. I mean, I don't know what your ultimate plans are."

He watched her carefully. "My plans?"

"After all of this is over? Are you still going to leave to work with your brother in Florida? That's a long way from here."

"It is a long way."

"I'm not saying that you need to stay with me. I..." Her cheeks warmed. "This has been really great, getting to know you again."

"Good," he said. "Let's just enjoy what's between us for what it is. Hot sex and some good times. Everything else will sort itself out."

She felt the color drain from her face. "Yeah. Sure."

Ryan leaned back. "I have a question. Those jars, the djinn ones. Do you think they really exist somewhere or did you just make it up?"

Emma was still trying to recover from hearing that Ryan considered their relationship to be not much more than a fling. "It's fiction. But you already know that."

"Yeah, I forgot. Sorry." Ryan tensed. "You know, something suddenly feels really off to me."

That made two of them. "Like what?"

"Maybe I should swing past Charlotte's place and see if she's up to anything."

Emma crossed her arms over her chest and put a bit of distance between them. "Better not get too close or she'll try to seduce you again."

His expression stiffened. "Like she did the other day, right?"

"Right." She pushed away her disappointment. She could deal with all of that later.

He finally got to his feet. His jeans looked dark in the half light of the room. "I need to go."

She looked at him with surprise. "You're going to leave me here? Just like that?"

"I'll be back."

This didn't sound like the plan they'd had earlier. She didn't blame Ryan for being impatient. She could, however, blame him for many other things at the moment.

Emma nodded. "Go ahead and do whatever you've got to do."

"How about a kiss for good luck?" he whispered, just before pulling her closer and pressing his mouth to hers. She wasn't surprised that she didn't feel anything this time. No lust or even a spark of desire. The Desidero potion was definitely a thing of the past.

Emma pulled back from him and he turned toward the door just as it swung open in front of them. Standing there was Ryan's exact double. His face was flushed red with anger and his hand clenched into tight fists at his sides.

"I'm going to kill you," he growled just before he stormed into the house and grabbed hold of Ryan.

Emma shrieked, clamping a hand over her mouth. She was stunned by what she was seeing. They were exactly the same. The clothes, the hair, the body, the face. Everything.

The real thief had used a potion in order to look like Ryan. To impersonate him. To pin the crime easily on him. And he was back for more. He looked *exactly* like Ryan.

The two Ryans fought on the floor, punching and clawing at each other. She'd already lost track of which man was the real Ryan.

There was a thunder of footsteps and suddenly Charlotte appeared at the door, wide-eyed as she looked in.

"Emma! I stopped by to make sure you were okay. What the hell's going on?"

This night was not going according to plan, to say the very damn least. Emma tried to breathe normally, but it was a struggle. She had to keep her wits about her or everything was going to fall completely apart. This wasn't how she planned to catch a thief—or two—but she had to roll with the punches.

"Stop this!" She surged forward and grabbed the bicep of one of the men. "I mean it. Stop this right now!"

They broke apart, scrambling back from each other.

"So do you see now?" one growled at her. "I was right all along."

Emma studied his face. She studied both of them, side by side, quickly, trying to spot any clues, any differences. They were dressed similarly, but not completely identical. One black T-shirt was slightly worn, a little more charcoal than gray. One pair of jeans was darker than the other. But everything else, down to the fine hair on their forearms, looked identical. Eyebrows, lips, eye color. They were like twins.

She couldn't help but snort. "Maybe you were wrong,

Ryan. Maybe this has nothing to do with a potion. Maybe you have a twin brother you weren't aware of."

"No," both said at the same time, then glared at each other.

The Ryan with the darker shirt stepped forward. "This son of a bitch attacked me outside and threw me in the trunk of my car. I tried to call you but it went to voicemail."

Emma regarded him cautiously. "If you say so."

He hissed out a breath. "Oh, come on, Em. You have to know it's really me."

Emma tried to think. "We'll just wait here until the potion wears off. Then whoever is lying will be revealed."

"Good idea," Ryan said.

"Bad idea," the other Ryan said. "By then, he'll have figured out a way to escape," he said, pointing to the other man. "If he's willing to steal and knock me unconscious, he's willing to do anything, especially when forced into a corner like a trapped animal."

Light-shirted Ryan eyed him. "You think so, huh? That's exactly what a criminal would say."

"Blow me." Dark-shirted Ryan rolled his eyes and looked directly at her. "I know we look alike, but can you seriously not see the difference? Come on."

"It'll be okay, Emma, I promise," Light-shirted Ryan said. "I'm here for you."

Emma frowned. "A couple minutes ago, you gave me the impression you were out of Mystic Ridge the moment you had the chance."

"I didn't say that."

"It was implied."

Dark-shirted Ryan glared at him. "If you insist on

impersonating me, the least you can do is not be a total dick about it."

The other Ryan clenched his fists. "You have no idea what you're talking about. You're going to pay for this."

"I already have," dark-shirted Ryan said. "I've paid with the last six months of my life."

"I can tell the difference," Charlotte added suddenly. "I can understand why you can't, Emma, but it's clear to me. After all, I was involved with Ryan for much longer than you were. Plus, I'm empathic."

Emma eyed her skeptically. "Okay, so tell me. Which is the real Ryan?"

She walked toward them, her gaze raking their bodies each in turn. She put her hand against one's chest, then did the same to the other.

"I didn't ask you to fondle them," Emma said with annoyance. "I asked you to tell me which one is the real Ryan."

"Sorry." Charlotte grinned. "I was having a personal fantasy there for a moment. I think I get why you wrote that book now."

"Sure you do."

Charlotte glanced at her with confusion. "I sense that you're angry with me."

Happy thoughts only. "Why would I be angry? You knew I was in a hard spot so you stopped by to make sure I was okay. That was really nice of you."

Charlotte returned her attention to the job at hand, sliding her fingers through both men's hair. Each one looked uncomfortable with the close scrutiny.

"It's this one." Charlotte put her hand on the lighter-shirted Ryan's shoulder.

"Yeah?" Emma asked, peering at him closer.

"No doubt about it."

"How do you know?"

Charlotte shrugged. "I just know."

That made two of them. Although Emma had already known the truth of who the real Ryan was for a while.

Charlotte was an empath and empaths couldn't sense the feelings of other empaths. Stephen—if this was Stephen in disguise—was a clairvoyant like Emma. His emotions would be bubbling up, ready for any empath to latch on to without much difficulty. But he could be hiding those feelings, especially if he thought Charlotte had cheated on him with Ryan...

She decided to continue to play along.

"I just wish I *knew*," Emma said, twisting a finger into her hair. "I mean, I thought that me and Ryan...the *real* Ryan...had something together. But if I can't tell the difference..."

She moved closer to lighter-shirted Ryan, placed her hands on his chest and looked up into his eyes. "Is it really you?"

"Yes, Emma. It's me."

"Em," the real Ryan growled from next to her. "What the hell? I can't believe you really don't know."

He sounded totally pissed. She was very glad to know he cared.

"I know now." She kept looking at light-shirted Ryan and pushed a very natural smile onto her face. "See, Ryan? It's going to be okay. Just like in my book, this is all going to have a happy ending."

He embraced her. "I'm so glad to hear that. Every story deserves a happily-ever-after."

"Uh, Em," the other Ryan said. "Your book didn't have a happy ending."

"I know." She leaned over to grab her gun out of the

purse she'd brought back downstairs with her earlier and pressed it into the side of the fake Ryan. "I think that's enough affection for one night, jerk."

He let go of her immediately, raising his hands, and backed up a step. "Shit."

"Yes, I'm armed. I'm dangerous. And I'm seriously pissed off."

"She definitely is," Ryan said. She glanced over her shoulder to see that he held Charlotte tightly by her wrist. "Nice of you to figure it out, by the way. I'm not insulted at all that it was that difficult."

She waved a hand. "Please. I knew it from the very beginning."

"You did?"

"Well…not the very beginning, but pretty damn close. He kept calling me Emma. Besides, he doesn't kiss anything like you do."

Ryan growled. "He kissed you? Son of a bitch."

His twin shrugged. "So sue me."

"I think I just might."

Somebody knocked on the frame of the open door. Emma looked over to see Patrick McKay standing there leaning on his cane. She was both surprised and relieved to see her agency manager at eleven-thirty on a Saturday night.

"Am I interrupting anything?" he asked calmly. Obviously, the scene in front of him didn't even merit a raised eyebrow.

Emma looked at Ryan.

He shrugged. "I called him before I came to rescue you. I'd hoped he'd believe the bizarre story I was about to tell him."

"I didn't believe you," Patrick said. "But it's been a slow night."

He entered the house and moved toward the false Ryan who looked severely dismayed by this turn of events. Patrick cocked his head to the side. "Doppelganger potion. Had I been the witness to your break and enter last year, I would have been able to tell immediately that you weren't really Ryan. Videotape isn't any good to an empath. Hello, Stephen. I'm guessing that your assessment and raise a few months ago weren't quite to your liking?"

Stephen just glared at his boss.

"Stephen?" Charlotte gasped. "My God. Is that really you? How could you do this? You're breaking my heart!"

"Can it, Charlotte," Patrick said. "It's now obvious to me what's happening. I think if I make a quick call to Xavier Franklin, he'd be very happy to tell me everything. Having PARA as a friend is much more beneficial to him than having us as an enemy. His secrets aren't quite as secret as he thinks they are."

Charlotte's eyes filled with tears. "This isn't fair. Emma, please, you have to believe that I never meant for things to go this far. The economy these days—"

"It's rough, I know." Emma nodded. "Stealing something and selling it for cold hard cash is really tempting when you're used to having money to burn all your life. I get it."

"And?" It was clear that Charlotte was looking for forgiveness.

"And—" Emma's grip on the gun was so tight, she was certain it would leave a mark. She just hoped nobody would guess that she never kept bullets in it. "—you can kiss my ass. I know it's not the most mature response, but it's been a long night. Sorry about that."

Patrick didn't call the police. He called the PARA board of directors.

Stephen and Charlotte looked at each other in misery. They knew dealing with the top brass would be much, much worse.

18

THE NIGHT WAS A BLUR. At the end of it, before they'd had much of a chance to talk everything out, Ryan headed back to his motel to gather up his belongings and Emma crashed for a couple hours of sleep. Patrick had asked to see both of them in his office first thing the next morning.

They arrived separately, but walked together to his office. The news of what had happened with Charlotte and Stephen wasn't yet common knowledge, so Ryan was met with glares by agents working the Sunday morning shift.

"It's okay," Emma said to him, reaching down to grab his hand. "It won't be much longer before everyone knows the truth."

"It's a relief," he said. "Can't lie about that."

"A celebration is in order."

"I totally agree."

"Come in." Patrick beckoned for them to enter his office. "Close the door."

They did as he asked and stood in front of his desk as he sorted through some paperwork. "Please, sit down."

There were two chairs across from him and they each

sat. Finally, Patrick folded his hands in front of him and looked across at Ryan, his expression somber.

"First of all, on behalf of myself and PARA, I want to extend my deepest apologies for the mistakes made six months ago. You were unjustly fired. I personally thought the evidence spoke for itself, but it goes to show that anyone can be fooled now and then."

The apology made Emma sigh in relief. It felt like it was a very long time coming. That it had all turned out for the best made her truly happy for Ryan.

Ryan nodded. "I appreciate that, Patrick. Honestly, if I'd been in your shoes, I would have done the same thing."

"Maybe, or maybe you would have take a little extra time, ignored the work piling up on your desk, and investigated a little deeper. Since you're an empath, I wasn't able to get a read on you. I realize just how much I rely on my ability to tell me who's lying and who's telling the truth. It wasn't an asset in this case. And for that I'm truly sorry."

Ryan reached across the desk and shook Patrick's hand. "I accept your apology. Thank you."

Emma grinned and rubbed his arm.

"Now, there's the matter of whether or not you'd be interested in coming back to PARA. You were a good agent."

Emma held her breath, waiting to hear his response. Maybe he'd stay in Mystic Ridge. With her. Ever since the fake Ryan had told her he wasn't interested in anything more than a fling, she'd been doubting what she and Ryan had. To her it was something special. Too bad she was a clairvoyant, not a mind reader.

"Thank you so much, Patrick." Ryan smiled. "I can't say I'm not tempted. In fact, if you'd asked me only a few weeks ago, I might have considered it. But too much has changed. I've changed. There are other paths for me to take."

Patrick nodded. "I completely understand. If you ever change your mind, just know there is a place for you here."

Emma's throat burned and she swallowed hard. "Patrick, I'm wondering why you needed to see me too this morning. It sounds like this is more between the two of you."

Patrick regarded her. "You I *can* read, Emma. I sensed that you'd want to be here, to find out first-hand what Ryan's plans are and whether they'd include coming back here."

"Well, obviously that's not what's going to happen."

"No. It's not." Patrick stood up from his desk. "I have some other business to attend to. Please feel free to use my office to privately discuss any further matters you have. Take care, Ryan, wherever your path leads you. You too, Emma."

Emma frowned, confused by what he'd said. "Okay."

Patrick left them alone.

She studied the edge of the desk in front of her. "So I guess this is it, isn't it?"

"What?"

"You're going to Florida to work with your brother. I—I just want to say how great it was to see you again. And I'm sorry, just like Patrick is, for ever doubting you. You're a good man, Ryan. One of the best and I'm—" She cleared her throat and felt the sting of tears threatening to spill. "I'm going to miss you so much."

There was silence for a long moment before she finally looked up. He was staring at her with an unidentifiable expression on his face.

"What?" she asked.

"So that's it? Thanks for the fling, send me a postcard from Florida?"

She shook her head. "What else can there be?"

His lips curved. "You are something, you know that, Em?"

A frown creased her brow. "I'm sorry, I'm not really following."

He searched her face. "Just because I'm not coming to work at PARA, it doesn't mean I'm in any damn hurry to leave Mystic Ridge."

She blinked at him. "What?"

"My gut tells me that I'm meant to do something else for a living. I was sure it was working with my brother. It's a great opportunity. But…" He shook his head. "That was before I fell head over heels in love with you." He took her hands in his.

She swallowed hard, not believing her ears. "In love with me?"

"I thought that was kind of obvious."

"It… I… But last night you said…" She trailed off. Wait a minute. That hadn't been "her" Ryan. It had been the impostor who'd been cruel to her, making her feel as if he was in hurry to leave town. "You really want to be with me?"

Ryan laughed a little under his breath. "You're making me work damn hard for this, aren't you?"

"I'm not trying to be difficult, I'm just… I just don't—"

He captured her face between his hands and kissed her deeply. "I love you, Emma Black. You and I were meant to be together. It's inevitable, don't you see that?"

Her heart pounded so hard she could hear it in her ears. Her breath came fast and shallow. Her lips tingled from his kiss and her body ached for him to touch her, to make love to her again.

Still, she pulled back from him and frowned. "You're wrong, Ryan."

His expression fell. "I'm wrong?"

Emma walked to the door and opened it, glancing back at Ryan over her shoulder. He stared after her bleakly.

"Patrick," she called. "Can you come back here for a moment?"

The silence stretched between them until Patrick returned a few moments later.

"What is it?" he asked.

She inhaled deeply before exhaling. "I love working for PARA but—but I need to give you my two week's notice."

He raised an eyebrow. "You're quitting your job?"

"Yes."

"May I ask why?"

She exhaled. "I think you already know why. You're empathic."

Patrick glanced over at Ryan who was staring at the both of them with an expression of complete and utter confusion on his face.

"What's going on here?" Ryan asked.

Patrick smiled. "You don't know? I knew your empathic abilities were a bit on the shaky side, but come on, Ryan. Really?"

Emma was a bit surprised as well. Ryan hadn't even tried to read her today. If he had, he'd likely know exactly how she was feeling.

Ryan looked at them each in turn. "You are both messing with me now, aren't you?"

"Maybe a little." Patrick's smile grew. "Let me spell it out for you. Emma is madly in love with you and she wants to quit her job so the two of you can be together."

Ryan's blue eyes widened. "Is that true?"

Emma grinned at him. "Well, not *totally* true. I mean, this isn't 1950 or anything. I have another book in my head so I'm going take the time to write it. I know that working with your brother is everything you've ever wanted and I refuse to let you give that up. So it's simple. You were willing to stay here for me. Well, I'm willing to go to Florida to be with you. That is, if—if you want me to."

He looked at her with shock before a smile spread across his face. "I want you to. So much."

"There's only one problem," Patrick said. "I don't accept your resignation."

Emma's grin faded and she stared at him. "What do you mean?"

"You're too good a clairvoyant. PARA needs you and I know you enjoy your job, even if you have other interests like writing. Walking away from your career is simply unacceptable."

She just gaped at him.

"So I propose a solution," he said. "I'll allow a six-month leave of absence for you to work on that book of yours and settle in down south."

"And then?" Emma asked.

"And then I'll expect you to start work at our Miami branch and see how you fit in." He smiled. "I think they'll appreciate you down there a great deal."

She stared at him, giving this news a chance to settle in. "I can't believe this."

"I hope that translates into, 'Thank you, Patrick. Excellent idea, Patrick.'"

She nodded slowly before a grin spread across her face. "Thank you, Patrick."

"Now if you'll excuse me." He nodded at them. "Good luck to you both. I always got the sense you two were meant to be together." He shrugged. "It was kind of inevitable, if you ask me."

Emma hugged Patrick tightly before he left the room again. Then she turned to face Ryan.

He was staring at her with surprise. "So, *that* was kind of unexpected."

"What part?"

"All of it." He drew her closer, his gaze moving over her features as if memorizing them. "You want to be with me."

"Yes." Emma placed her hands on his chest and looked up into his handsome face, trying to gauge how he was feeling at the moment. "Are you okay with this?"

"You coming with me to Florida to start a new life together?"

She watched him warily. "Yes. That is, if you want me to."

He cocked his head. "I'm okay with it on one condition."

She tensed. "What's that?"

"Patrick's the one who just told me how you feel. But I'd really like to hear it from you, just to make sure it's actually true."

Tears welled in her eyes. She nodded and slid her arms around his waist. "I love you, Ryan Shephard. I love you. I love you. I love you. How's that?"

He grinned and pulled her closer to him. "That's a pretty good start. But I'll probably need to hear it a few billion more times."

Emma laughed. "I think that can be arranged."

"So when exactly does this new future together begin?"

She pulled his face down to hers and kissed him. "The sooner the better."

His grin widened. "Just what I was thinking."

"It's almost like we're psychic or something." She grinned at him.

"Okay, so what am I thinking right now?" He raised an eyebrow.

"Mr. Shephard, I believe I've written that scene a few times before. Very naughty."

"Why, thank you." He looked down at her, his expression growing serious again. "I love you, Emma. Now let's get the hell out of here. There's a couple more scenes from that book of yours that I'd really like to explore."

She eyed him. "My book without the happy ending, you mean."

"We'll really have to work on that."

"You know, I'm suddenly extremely inspired to write a better ending next time."

"I can't tell you how glad I am to hear that." He kissed her and fresh desire surged inside of her.

Patrick was right. It had been inevitable that she and Ryan would find each other again. They'd been great partners, working together like a well-oiled machine. She'd liked him before she loved him. She *still* liked him. Deeply. Madly. Desperately.

A lust potion had driven them into each other's arms, despite everything that might have kept them apart.

Now the masks had been discarded once and for all. The potion's effects had dissipated. But the desire they felt for each other was stronger than ever.

She'd wasted too much time trusting her eyes. Now

she trusted her heart. And her gut. They were two things that didn't lie.

She never believed in happy endings. But this man had more than proved to her that happy endings were real.

And maybe she could even write one or two of them....

Ryan loved her. And she loved him.

Forget happy endings. For them, this was a fantastic beginning.

* * * * *

COMING NEXT MONTH

Available March 29, 2011

#603 SECOND TIME LUCKY
Spring Break
Debbi Rawlins

#604 HIGHLY CHARGED!
Uniformly Hot!
Joanne Rock

#605 WHAT MIGHT HAVE BEEN
Kira Sinclair

#606 LONG SLOW BURN
Checking E-Males
Isabel Sharpe

#607 SHE WHO DARES, WINS
Candace Havens

#608 CAUGHT ON CAMERA
Meg Maguire

HBCNM0311

REQUEST YOUR FREE BOOKS!
2 FREE NOVELS PLUS 2 FREE GIFTS!

red-hot reads!

YES! Please send me 2 FREE Harlequin® Blaze® novels and my 2 FREE gifts (gifts are worth about $10). After receiving them, if I don't wish to receive any more books, I can return the shipping statement marked "cancel." If I don't cancel, I will receive 6 brand-new novels every month and be billed just $4.24 per book in the U.S. or $4.71 per book in Canada. That's a saving of at least 15% off the cover price. It's quite a bargain. Shipping and handling is just 50¢ per book in the U.S. and 75¢ per book in Canada.* I understand that accepting the 2 free books and gifts places me under no obligation to buy anything. I can always return a shipment and cancel at any time. Even if I never buy another book, the two free books and gifts are mine to keep forever.

151/351 HDN FC4T

Name _____ (PLEASE PRINT)

Address _____ Apt. #

City _____ State/Prov. _____ Zip/Postal Code

Signature (if under 18, a parent or guardian must sign)

Mail to the **Reader Service:**
IN U.S.A.: P.O. Box 1867, Buffalo, NY 14240-1867
IN CANADA: P.O. Box 609, Fort Erie, Ontario L2A 5X3

Not valid for current subscribers to Harlequin Blaze books.

Want to try two free books from another line?
Call 1-800-873-8635 or visit www.ReaderService.com.

* Terms and prices subject to change without notice. Prices do not include applicable taxes. Sales tax applicable in N.Y. Canadian residents will be charged applicable taxes. Offer not valid in Quebec. This offer is limited to one order per household. All orders subject to credit approval. Credit or debit balances in a customer's account(s) may be offset by any other outstanding balance owed by or to the customer. Please allow 4 to 6 weeks for delivery. Offer available while quantities last.

Your Privacy—The Reader Service is committed to protecting your privacy. Our Privacy Policy is available online at www.ReaderService.com or upon request from the Reader Service.

We make a portion of our mailing list available to reputable third parties that offer products we believe may interest you. If you prefer that we not exchange your name with third parties, or if you wish to clarify or modify your communication preferences, please visit us at www.ReaderService.com/consumerschoice or write to us at Reader Service Preference Service, P.O. Box 9062, Buffalo, NY 14269. Include your complete name and address.

HBI I

*Selene wanted nothing to do with the father of her son,
Alex; but Aristedes had other plans...that included them.*

*Read on for an sneak peek from
THE SARANTOS SECRET BABY by Olivia Gates,
available April 2011, only from Harlequin Desire.*

"You were right to turn my marriage offer down," Aristedes said.

And Selene found her voice at last, found the words that
would not betray the blow he'd dealt her. "Thanks for letting
me know. You didn't have to come all the way here,
though. You could have just let it go. I left yesterday with
the understanding that this case is closed."

Before the hot needles behind her eyes could dissolve
into an unforgivable display of stupidity and weakness, she
began to close the door.

The door stopped against an immovable object. His flat palm.

"I can't accept that." His voice was low, leashed.

What did her tormentor mean now? Was he ending one
game only to start another?

She raised eyes as bruised as her self-respect to his,
found nothing there but solemnity and determination.

Before she could voice her confusion, he elaborated. "I
never let anything go unless I'm certain it's unworkable. I
realize I made you an unworkable offer, and that's why I'm
withdrawing it. I'm here to offer something else. A workability
study."

She leaned against the door, thankful for its support and
partial shield. "Your son and I are not a business venture
you can test for feasibility."

His gaze grew deeper, made her feel as if he was trying
to delve into her mind, take control of it. "It's actually the

other way around. I'm the one who would be tested."

She shook her head. "Why bother? I know—and *you* know—you're not workable. Not with me."

His spectacular eyebrows lowered over eyes she felt were emitting silver hypnosis. "You're right again. Neither you nor I have any reason to believe that isn't the truth. The only truth. It might be best for both you and Alex to never hear from me again, to forget I exist. But then again, maybe not. I'm only asking for the chance for both of us to find out for certain. You believe I'm unworkable in any personal relationship. I've lived my life based on that belief about myself. I never really had reason to question it. But I have one now. In fact, I have two."

Find out what happens in
THE SARANTOS SECRET BABY by Olivia Gates,
available April 2011, only from Harlequin Desire.

Harlequin® Blaze™
red-hot reads

Sunny, sensual Hawaiian spring break…again!

Three best girlfriends are recapturing an amazing spring-break vacation they had a decade ago.

First on the beach is former attorney and all-around good girl Mia Butterfield. Meeting up with her boyfriend of old is a bust, so she's shocked when her hero turns out to be someone she'd never have expected…

Find out who it is in
SECOND TIME LUCKY
by acclaimed author
Debbi Rawlins

Available from Harlequin Blaze® April 2011

Part of the sensual miniseries,
Spring Break

Part 2: Delicious Do-Over (May)